All Hands on

Death

DEVIN SCHLOTTMAN

PAGE PUBLISHING
Conneaut Lake, PA

First originally published by Page Publishing 2024

ISBN 979-8-89157-956-9 (pbk)
ISBN 979-8-89157-973-6 (digital)

Printed in the United States of America

CHAPTER 1

THE AFTERNOON AIR IS BITTER cold. Streetlights swing rapidly in the heavy, freezing wind. The warm sun disappears behind the clouds, and the air becomes more frigid. Jay Johnson walks quickly across the parking lot, hood up, gloves tight, and a scarf wrapped around his face. He holds a briefcase in one hand, while the other is tucked away in his coat pocket. Jay opens the door to his Ram truck, gets in, and fires up the engine. The inside of the truck is so cold that he can see his breath. Body shivering, Jay puts his hands up to the warm air vent. Frost from the windows begins to disappear. When his body is at a comfortable temperature, Jay puts his truck in gear and pulls out of the parking lot, leaving Al's Accounting. Carefully cruising home on the frozen roads, Jay listens to 80.7 AM. Ice cracks under the weight of his truck as he races down the street. As he passes the intersection, Jay turns down the heater, as it makes him feel sleepy.

At a red light, Jay flips down his visor mirror and looks at himself. Big, dark circles cover the bottom of his eyes. *I'll take a nap when I get home*, Jay thinks.

After about fifteen minutes of driving, Jay pulls into the driveway next to the parked Chevy Silverado. Jogging through the bone-chilling air, Jay runs through the front door. His body shivers as he takes off his coat and shoes. "Carly, I'm home!" Jay shouts throughout the warm house. The sound of footsteps comes running down the stairs. A good-looking brunette with a tall, curvy body appeared in front of him.

"Hey, handsome," Carly said before placing a kiss on his cheek.

1

"Afternoon, good-looking," Jay replied with a blush.

"How was your day?" Carly asked.

"Fine. Just happy to be home," Jay said.

Jay walks into the living room and sits down on the couch by the fire. He turns on the TV and covers himself with a blanket as he puts his feet up. After surfing through the channels, Carly announces that dinner is ready. Jay gets out of his chair and walks over to the dinner table. Carly places a steaming plate of steak and mashed potatoes in front of him with a side of steak sauce. She also brings him a bottle of Miller Lite. Carly then makes a plate for herself and sits down next to Jay.

After a while, Jay does not have much to say. He has been very quiet since he got home. Carly puts her fork down and looks at him.

"Is something bothering you, hon?" she asks.

Jay, who was chewing a piece of steak, stops and takes a sip of Miller Lite. He, too, puts his fork on the side of his plate.

"I don't know," he said. "Just lately, I felt overwhelmed. I've been up to my neck in paperwork. Tax returns are a bitch. Hell, I even found a few gray hairs the other day."

"Well, maybe you should take some time off, you know? Go and do something."

Jay sits back in his chair and considers what Carly suggested. He rakes his hair back. He then leans forward, taking another sip of Miller Lite.

"I don't see why not. You and I could do something."

Carly smiles a little. "Like a getaway?" she asks.

"Yeah," Jay says excitedly. "Let's go somewhere. Have an adventure together."

Carly gets out of her chair and walks over to her desk. She rather quickly flips through a stack of papers and returns to her husband with a pamphlet. The pamphlet shows an offer for a one-week cruise around the Pacific ocean. Jay reads over each description with a little smile.

"You wanna do this?" he asks.

"Yeah! Ever since I was little, I've wanted to go on one," Carly says.

Jay looks at the pamphlet again.

"Not a bad price. Hundred and thirty bucks for the whole week. Plus, I know once we get there, you're gonna spend all my money."

Carly's jaw drops, and she playfully smacks him on the shoulder. Jay snickers. Jay then picks up the phone, and within a few minutes, he hangs up with a smile on his face. They are set for the cruise. They celebrate with a few kisses.

Later that night, Jay stands at the bathroom sink, brushing his teeth. As he brushes his teeth, Carly showers behind the curtain. Jay spits in the sink and accidentally runs the water.

"Hey! That's cold!" Carly says.

Jay laughs.

"Sorry. If you don't mind, I'm going to flush the toilet now."

"Jay! If you do, I'll punch you in the dick as hard as I can," Carly says.

"Carly, you wouldn't do that. You love me too much."

Carly pokes her head out of the shower. "Try me." Carly pulls her head back in the shower. Jay exits the bathroom and lies in bed. He grabs the book off the nightstand and begins to read. After a few pages, Carly is still in the bathroom.

"Carly? You okay?" Jay asks from the bed.

"Yeah, I'm okay. I got a surprise for you."

Jay puts his book down.

Carly slowly opens the bathroom door. Jay is happy with what he sees. Carly stands in the doorway, one arm leaning against the wall. She is only wearing a G-string. Jay is aroused. Carly begins a slow, sexy catwalk toward him. She then lies on top of Jay.

"I know you've been stressed out lately. Why don't I help you with that?"

"I'd really like that," Jay says in a low, deep whisper.

Carly slowly drags her hand down Jay's body until her hand is down his pants. Her hand grips firmly around his erection. Jay grabs her butt, pulls her in, and presses his lips against hers. After some smooth kissing, Carly pulls down Jay's underwear. She teases him by going really slow at first, then making a fast jerking motion.

Soon Carly is on her back, throwing her head side to side on the pillow. Every few seconds, she yells, "Yes, yes!" Jay has Carly on her stomach, her ass pushed back in the air. As he pumps harder and harder each time, he smacks Carly's ass, making her moan louder and louder each time. After a long hour of intense intercourse, both finish with amazing, pleasurable orgasms. Jay rolls over on his back. They are both out of breath, sweaty, and happy. Jay looks at Carly.

"What did you do at the end?" Jay asks.

Carly put her hands over her face.

"I don't know. I kinda just did it," she says.

CHAPTER 2

A FEW DAYS AFTER THEIR long night of intercourse, Jay and Carly wake up early on the day of the cruise. Carly makes breakfast while Jay finishes packing. Jay packs some shorts, short-sleeve shirts, sunscreen, and different kinds of Hawaiian shirts.

Before they leave the house, Jay and Carly eat breakfast, then make sure everything is taken care of. For the time being, they take their winter coats off the rack and head outside to Jay's Ram truck. Carly puts the bags in the back, and Jay puts the location in the GPS. He then starts the truck and backs out of the driveway.

A few minutes into the drive, Jay grabs Carly's hand. Her hand feels cold. Lifting her hand to his mouth, Jay plants a kiss on the back of it. She looks at him, smiles, then puts her head back.

"Are you excited?" Jay asks.

"Yeah," Carly says as she yawns. "I'm very excited. And I'm a little worried."

Jay looks confused.

"Worried about what?" he asks.

"I don't know exactly. I just have this feeling that something is going to happen. Like something goes wrong, but then it'll be okay."

"What are you afraid of?" Jay asks. "Not having a good time? That you'll lose me in a crowd? Getting the shits when you're too far away from the room?"

Carly looks at him with a look he's gotten many, many times.

"Okay, first, gross. Second, I know you and I will be together the whole time. I just really don't know, Jay."

"Well, you know I'll be right next to you. I have a little friend in the side of my bag."

"You brought your gun?" Carly asks.

"Yes, ma'am."

"Please be careful with it. Don't do anything stupid."

No answer from Jay. After a while, Carly ends up falling asleep. Jay turns off the radio and focuses on driving. Driving down the highway on Route 1, Jay looks up at the sky. The sun begins to peak over the horizon, taking over the night sky clouds. There is a hint of orange mixed in with a little blue color. The view takes Jay's breath away.

The forty-five-minute drive comes to an end. Jay pulls his Ram into a parking lot, puts the truck in park, and kills the engine. Gently shaking her shoulder, he wakes Carly. She rubs her eyes and stretches. Jay pokes her in the belly. She playfully smacks his hand away. They get out of the car, get their bags, and stand to admire the ship. Carly squeezes Jay's hand. The air is warm, and the smell of salt water fills their lungs. This gives Carly butterflies. The couple shares a long kiss.

As everyone crowds onto the ship, seagulls fly overhead, and waves cause the ship to rock back and forth slightly. This causes Carly to grab hold of Jay's arm. "It's okay," he says. "Just a little rocking." Slowly, they walk toward the center of the ship. Around them are waiters and attendants.

A young man, who looked no older than twenty-five, approaches Jay and Carly. He is dressed in a bright white uniform shirt. He has slightly long hair, and scruff covers his face.

"Welcome aboard, folks," the young man says. "May I see your tickets?"

Jay puts his hands into his pockets and gasps while turning to Carly. "What? Did you forget them!" she yells at him.

Jay laughs, pulls the tickets out of his pocket, and hands them to the young man. He looks at them and shakes his head. Carly smacks his arm and smiles.

"Dickhead," she says quietly to him.

"Mr. and Mrs. Johnson?" the attendant asks.

"Yes, sir," Jay says.

"Ah, wonderful. May I take your bags?"

"Oh, yeah, sure," Carly says, still smirking.

"Great. Let me show you to your room."

The young man grabs their bags and escorts Jay and Carly to their room. They are there for a short walk.

"Have you folks ever been on a cruise ship before?" the young man asks.

"No," Carly says. "Very first time."

"Oh, well then, welcome aboard the *Wave Crusher*."

"The *Wave Crusher*?" Jay asks with a surprised look.

The young man shakes his head, as in, yeah, I know. "Yeah, silly name for a ship, right? But what can ya do?" He sticks out his hand. "I'm Jack, by the way."

"Nice to meet you, Jack. I'm Jay. This is my wife, Carly."

Jack then fishes a card from his pocket. A click sound escapes from the door, and the little red light turns green. "Alrighty, Mr. Johnson. Here's your room key. If you lose it, just head down to the front desk. They'll give you an extra. I hope you two enjoy your stay. If you need anything, please don't hesitate to ask."

"Thank you very much, Jack," Jay says, pulling a five-dollar bill from his pocket. Jack hesitates. Then he takes the money. He leaves Jay and Carly by themselves.

Carly opens the curtain, letting the sun shine through the windows. She flops on the bed, spreading her body out. Jay rubs his hand up her leg, slowly inching toward her private area. Carly shoves her bare foot in his face and waves her finger.

"No touching," she says.

Jay frowns. "Aww."

Jay crawls next to her in bed. Carly lies by her side. Jay lies on his side behind her, holding her in his arms. One hand is in her pants, holding her butt. Jay turns Carly's head toward him and gives her a kiss. Jay cuddles her closer in his arms. Soon they are sound asleep.

It is around seven o'clock when Jay and Carly wake up. The lovebirds change and get ready for the ship's evening party on the deck.

When they get to the party, they sit at the minibar and order two Miller Lites. A few passengers are up dancing and having a good time. Carly looks at Jay and says, "We should dance."

"Uh, I'm not drunk enough yet. Maybe later."

"Jay. I'm not stupid. I know that 'later' will never come."

Jay smiles. "You know me so well."

Carly smacks him on the shoulder.

The night starts to go by. Soon, it will be nine at night. Jay and Carly are sitting on deck chairs. Jay is on his third beer. And Carly knows that when Jay drinks too much, he tends to get a little handsy. She likes when Jay gets handsy with her in public, but only at certain times and places he touches her.

While they are talking, Jay is accidentally bumped into. A man with a barrel chest turns around. "Oh, shit. I'm sorry, man."

"No worries," Jay says.

The man sticks out his hand while holding a beer in the other. "I'm Dustin."

"Jay. This is my wife, Carly."

"Hey, you happen to have seen a guy who's wearing a neon shirt? Long hair with a five o'clock shadow?" Dustin asks.

Jay shakes his head. "No, I haven't."

"Shit. I swear he has the attention span of a nat. Sometimes it's hard working with him. I always gotta hunt him down."

"Oh, you work with him?" Carly asks.

Dustin sits down. "Yeah. We're both police officers. We happened to be on vacation at the same time. If you don't mind me asking, what do you folks do for a living?"

Jay takes another sip of his beer, then suffers Carly's stare. "What?" he says. "I paid for it. Of course, I'm gonna finish it." Dustin gives a little chuckle. "Anyways, I'm an accountant. Carly's a wedding planner. She actually planned our wedding."

"Oh, that's interesting," Dustin says. "Where'd you guys get married?"

"Florida," Carly says.

"Very nice. I always wanted to go there."

"Are you married?" Jay asks.

"Widow…" Dustin says in a low voice.

"I'm sorry to hear that," Carly says. "If you don't mind me asking, what happened?"

"She uh…had breast cancer." Dustin clears his throat, wiping his eyes with the hand holding his beer.

"I'm sorry to hear that, man," Jay says.

Dustin lightly shakes his head. "Thank you. I mean, hey, she's free. She doesn't have to suffer anymore."

The next minute is silent. Jay has felt bad for asking and is tempted to drink, only to realize that his bottle is empty. He thinks about ordering another. But he doesn't want Carly to be pissed off on their vacation.

They shoot the bull for ten minutes when a tall man in a neon shirt approaches Dustin. He introduces himself as John to Jay and Carly. Just by looking at him, Carly can tell John, like Jay, has one too many. Dustin leans forward, looking at John. "John, what happened to your face?"

John rubs his cheek. "Oh, there was this hot girl over by the pool. I talked to her, then I grabbed her ass. She smacked me."

Dustin runs a hand down his face. "Jesus Christ, John. Why do I have to babysit you all the time?"

"Relax, Dustin. Just a little buzzed."

Dustin huffs. "When are you gonna sing a different song?" Dustin gets up from his seat. "It was nice meeting you two. John, come back to the room sober, or don't come back at all."

As Dustin vanishes into the night, John leans against the mini-bar. His breath has a strong stench of alcohol. Carly looks at him and says, "Well, it serves you right to have been slapped. Lucky, she didn't punch you."

"Or throw you overboard," Jay adds.

"Yeah. I can be an ass. Dustin hasn't been the same since his wife died. Poor thing. She didn't see it coming."

"Sadly, yes. Breast cancer can be really fatal."

John looks up. "What are you talking about?" he asks.

"What are *you* talking about?" Carly asks.

John doesn't say anything; he only stares at Jay and Carly. His face is blank, but there is a small wave of fear rolling around in John's eyes. He raises his beer bottle in the air. "I've said too much. You folks have a good night."

Jay and Carly are left sitting, confused.

CHAPTER 3

DUSTIN SITS ON THE EDGE of the bed, tears soaking into his cheeks. Every time he attempts to clear his mind of those horrible images, his brain fails to block them. He inhales, then exhales, trying to calm himself down.

The attempt fails.

He decides that maybe a shower will calm his nerves. Waiting for the water to warm, Dustin stands motionless. Suddenly, he feels an overwhelming burning sensation in his stomach. Dashing for the toilet, Dustin closes his eyes and lets his body take over. His throat is as hot as fire.

When it's over, he flushes the toilet and gets in the shower. Only a few seconds after the water hits his body, Dustin sits in a ball on the tub floor, sobbing.

Jay and Carly lie soundly asleep. It is nearly four o'clock in the morning. Carly begins to dream. In her dream, Carly is by herself, walking in what looks like a dark room. She has a difficult time figuring things out. Her vision is blurry.

As she dreams, Jay rolls on his side and puts his warm hand on Carly's breast. He slowly makes his way down until he is touching her. Though she is sleeping, Carly can feel her husband's hand. She thinks about smacking it away, but she focuses on her dream.

Carly sees an odd event. She sees a woman who appears to be floating. Something is underneath her. Due to the blurriness, Carly can't tell what it is. Suddenly, she's in another bedroom. She still can't make out the scene. Carly starts to move around as if she were scared.

Jay pulls his hand out, thinking it was beginning to bother her. Carly pushes back. Jay is getting worried.

Carly is scared awake. She almost falls out of bed until Jay grabs her and holds her in his arms. "Are you okay?" he asks. Carly's face is covered in sweat, and her breathing is heavy. She dashes for the bathroom, turns on the sink, and runs water over her face. She holds herself up on the counter, letting the water drip off her chin.

"Baby, what happened?" Jay asks. Carly wiped away the water with her hand.

"I don't know," she says, huffing. "Must have just been a very bad nightmare."

"About what?"

"I'm not exactly sure. Everything was blurry."

"That's weird," Jay says, looking at his watch. "It's still early. You wanna try to sleep?"

"I think I'm gonna stay up."

Jay climbs back into bed. He covers himself with a blanket and puts his head on the soft pillow. As her husband falls back to sleep, Carly sits on her side of the bed. Brushing her hair back and rubbing her face, she asks herself, *What was that dream about? What the hell happened?*

At seven in the morning, Jay wakes up, rubbing his eyes. He finds Carly in the bathroom, drying her hair from a shower. Jay throws the comforter to the side, jumping out of bed. Grabbing her by the hips, he pulls her in and kisses her on the neck.

"How ya feeling?" he asks.

"Okay," Carly says. "Still a little freaked out."

Jay kisses her on the cheek. "You'll be okay, baby. A day of relaxation should help." Carly does not reply.

Passengers on board eat, drink, and talk among themselves. At the helm of the ship stands a tall, slim man. His hands are behind his back, and his stance is perfectly erect. He is clean-shaven, has a short haircut, and is nearly bald. He wears his uniform perfectly; there is not a crease to be found.

"Good morning," he shouts. "I am Captain West! First, welcome aboard the *Wave Crusher*! We hope you have an amazing time.

If there is anything you need on my left, it is my staff—Jack, Chad, and Cindy. Thank you again for boarding with us, and have a good time, everyone!"

Captain West walks out of sight, probably back to his office. Passengers party until the sun goes to sleep. Tired children are put to bed, and parents and couples prepare for the night.

CHAPTER 4

THE STARS APPEAR HIGH IN the sky. Cold chills roll through the wind, waves break apart at the nose of the ship, and water trickles down the sides. Everyone but a few members of the crew sleep soundly in bed. As the ship shreds through the water, the wind starts to pick up. Chairs on the deck dance with the wind. Umbrellas hang on for dear life.

Captain West is sound asleep in bed when he is awakened by a loud bang. A wave of heat forces his pores to tense. Orange flames engulf the floor beneath his feet. He rushes to throw on his robe and run to the control room. Two of the crew members, Daniel and Mike, frantically try to keep the out-of-control ship steady.

"What the fuck is going on in here!" West yells.

"Ship's out of control, Captain! We can't override it because the systems are down!" Mike yells. "The weather's starting to get really fucking bad!"

As the ship gets pummeled by waves, everyone is woken up by the commotion, dazed and confused. Little do they know what is happening. Items fly all over the place. Glass breaks, lights flicker on and off, and children begin to scream bloody murder.

From the impact of the intense storm, water pours through the broken windows. Adrenaline pumps, hearts pound, husbands hold their wives tight, and women with children hold them close to their chest. They do what they can to protect their cubs. In the control room, Captain West, Daniel, and Mike begin to panic. Captain West grabs the microphone from the intercom.

"Everyone, remain calm! Protect yourselves as best you can!" he yells.

Mike and Daniel have a thousand-yard stare. They grip the wheels that steer the ship. "What the hell is that?" Mike asks. Off in the distance, there appears to be a small area of trees and sand. The *Wave Crusher* is approaching at top speed. Captain West holds the microphone in his mouth.

"Brace for impact!"

The *Wave Crusher* comes to a sudden, hard stop. Shelves of books, deck chairs, tables, pictures, glass, food in the kitchen, TVs, and papers fly forward, straight ahead, not caring who or what it hits. Screams echo through the ship—cries of pain. The nose of the ship makes a loud, popping crunch. A huge crack comes from an unknown location. Water engulfs the *Wave Crusher*. People who are screaming get a mouth full of water. A woman who does not fully follow Captain West's orders is thrown back on the wall of her room, causing her to smack her head, drawing blood and leaking into the paint and cool sea water, taking her life.

Captain West finds himself fully submerged in the water. He swims over to Mike and Daniel. Captain West sees that the impact is enough to end their time on earth. With one breath left in his lungs, Captain West paddles as fast as he can to find the surface. Fish from the outside find themselves joining the frightened passengers, swimming in all directions. Captain West wishes he had a set of gills right now.

He knows this ship like the back of his hand. He is down on the first floor by the dining room. Plates, silverware, and tables float freely. Captain West then discovers where the loud crack is coming from. The center of the ship is nearly split in two. That is his escape. His lungs start to burn, needing new air. Using all he has left, Captain West navigates his way out. From the corner of his eye, Captain West spots large bubbles. Then comes a water-muffled scream from a woman. Her feet are pinned under twisted and broken dining tables. He locks eyes with her. Though his lungs burn, Captain West will attempt to free her. First, he closes her mouth, preserving whatever air she has let. Then he goes to work on the wooden tables. Captain

West knows the impact of the tables has broken the woman's ankles. As he fights to get her ankles free, the woman begins to struggle. With one final push, Captain West breaks the table's legs. He wraps his arms around the woman and swims. A sudden burst of energy takes over his body. Finally, Captain West sees sunlight dancing on the water's surface. He bursts through the water, taking the biggest breath he can. He looks at the woman. She isn't moving. As he gets her to the beach, Captain West checks for a pulse. Nothing. With years of training, Captain West begins CPR. He counts out loud, "1, 2, 3, 4, 5, 6, 7, 8, 9, 10." He counts to thirty. Again, he checks. No pulse. Captain West performs CPR a second time. Then a third. And a fourth. Captain West balls up next to the woman. "I'm so sorry," he says. He wants to tell himself that he does everything he can, but that isn't enough.

After wiping the tears from his eyes, Captain West looks up at the horrific scene. Passengers continue to escape the crumbling ship. Some jump for their lives into the water on the other side. It appears that one passenger is using other people to keep himself afloat. Like a pack of wolves, a family prances on him. A tall male dives down, producing an older female, taking in a breath similar to that of Captain West a moment ago. That is when he witnesses a bunch of males and two females throwing punches at the man. He looks away. When he looks back up, one of the males says, "He's finished." The beaten man floats on his back while blood pours from his nose. Just a short distance away, several other passengers have lacerations on their arms and legs, along with a few on their faces. Captain West can't help but sit there like a child who can hear his parents arguing at a late hour. Staying balled up, Captain West observes everything. The whole situation is everything they have trained him for since he was a younger fella. In the beginning of this madness, Captain West has one question for himself. *Where do I start?*

Jay and Carly race to safety. When Jay opens the door, water rushes down the hall, forcing its way into their room. "You gotta hold your breath!" Jay says. As they swim for their lives, they witness other passengers frantically paddling to safety. A woman who appears to have no idea how to swim twists, jerks, and throws herself all around. Jay and Carly watch as the woman's body goes limp. There is nothing they can do to help her. She is dead. They swim until they hit the center of the ship. When they crawl on the dry sand, Jay notices that the ship has literally broken into two. The nose is parked on land, and the ass end sits halfway in the water. Jay pants like a tired dog. Carly is breathing heavily, but not as badly.

Dustin and John emerge from underwater. They swim to shore to meet the couple. "You guys okay?" Dustin asks.

"Yeah," Jay says. "What happened?"

Dustin shrugs. "Other than the ship that crashed, that's the best answer I can give ya."

All the remaining passengers regroup. Thankfully, all their loved ones are safe.

Several of the passengers have cuts and bruises. One man has a large gash down the side of his face. Due to his paleness, Dustin declares that the man is dead or will die shortly. He knows this way too well. Jay grabs a hold of Carly and examines her. There is not a scratch on her. *Thank God*, Jay thought.

Late in the morning, the wind grows colder, and everyone begins to shiver. Warm blankets are prepared and passed out. Food, along with medicine, is distributed. West and his staff work around the clock to make sure that everything and everyone is okay. Some of the passengers decide to walk around the island.

Despite the sun not rising, the sand is surprisingly warm. The water is a few degrees above freezing. Just by the look of it, the nose of the ship is beyond repair. West and his staff all agreed that the ship is irreplaceable.

West walks over to Jay's group. He kneels while running his hand on his shiny head. "You folks okay? Does anyone need anything? Food? Medicine?"

Everyone either said "no" or nodded.

"So, Captain," John says, "what happened?"

"The weather just took over. Two of my staff members in the control room did everything they could. Unfortunately, they couldn't keep the ship steady and didn't make it out. One said the system was down." West shakes his head. "Doesn't make sense. Everything on that ship worked perfectly fine."

Not a word is said for a long moment. The group sits huddled together, trying to keep warm. Carly shivers the most. Jay wraps his arms around her, pulling her close.

"Mr. West," Dustin breaks the silence. "How long do you think we'll be here?"

Captain West huffs. "My staff member Jack is trying to get a radio connection as we speak. We should be out of here sooner than you know."

"*Should?*" Carly asks.

"Yes," West says with authority. "*Should.*"

Off in the background is a familiar voice. It is the voice of Jack. He is waving West over. West and Jack then walk to a more private area.

"Captain. We have a problem," Jack says.

"What now?" West asks with a disappointed tone.

"I can't get shit on the radio."

West gives a frustrated huff. "What are we supposed to do?" he asks. "All those people are expecting us to call in a Mayday. And now we have to tell them that we have no way of doing it?"

Silence again fills the air. Then it hits Jack like a runaway train. "Wait a minute," he says. "The sat phone."

West's face lights up.

"Yes, but I seemed to have lost the one I had. It was in the safe when we crashed. And it's too dangerous to swim in open water this early."

"The control room!" Jack and West say simultaneously. Both men run to what is left of the second floor, hoping to gain access to the control room.

When they arrive, they find a gaping hole right above the control room. Water levels off their entry point. West has hoped they can get the sat phone, call for help, and get off the island. "The backup sat phone has to be in one of those drawers," West says.

"Great. How are we supposed to get it?" asks Jack.

"We dive down and get it," West replies.

"Is it even waterproof?" asks Jack.

West shrugs. "We're gonna find out." He is about to leap in.

Jack stops. Leaning forward, he focuses on the partially clear water. He thinks his mind is playing tricks on him. Jack grabs his arm. "Hold on, Captain. I think I see something."

"Where?"

Jack points. "There. It looks gray or dark tan."

The object starts moving. "What the fuck?" West mutters. A dorsal fin pops out and slices through the water.

Shark.

Not a big one, but big enough to tear you apart if it needs to or wants to. It must have snuck its way in. "Great!" Jack says, throwing his arms up. "How are we gonna get the fucking phone?"

Jack and West return to the island. Sounds of chatter flew. Soon those chatters will be a bunch of upset vacationers. West walks over to a large rock and sits with his head in his hands. Jack places his hand on his boss's shoulder.

"I know you're upset. But we can find a way to get it. We just have to wait until the shark swims away to get food. If we stay out of the water, it'll have no idea we're even here. We go find food on land and avoid fishing. At least for right now"

John approaches. "So what's your plan, Captain?"

West quickly informs John of the situation. "We need to stay out of the water and wait for the shark to leave. Then one of us can swim down and get the sat phone. Any volunteers?" Not a single hand flies in the air. Carly grabs Jay by the arm. "Are you crazy?" she says through her teeth. "You can't wait out a damn shark!"

"I'm not gonna take no for an answer. This is a dangerous and violent shark," Jay says.

"It's going to take forever. Who knows how long! It could be days or weeks, and I don't think we should just wait and do nothing," Carly tells her husband.

Jay breaks Carly's grip. He then holds her shoulder and looks deeply into her eyes. "Do you want to get off this island or not?" Carly says nothing. She then follows her husband along with the others.

West leads them to the control room. There is just enough room for all of them to stand. The water is ankle level. Small, tiny waves splash around.

There it is. One of the ocean's deadliest predators swims fearlessly, right where the group needs to get. Its dorsal fin rises from the water, indicating that this is his territory. The bull shark swims closer to them as they look at him.

"Alright," West says, "so we know where it is."

Dustin gives West the look he gives when you've just said something stupid. "Takers? Yeah, you're funny."

"I'm the captain."

"Last time I checked, the captain *of the ship* wasn't supposed to be a pussy when it comes to situations like this. Now get your ass down there and get that fucking sat phone. Or I will throw you down there and let the shark have an early dinner snack."

"Alright, you two," John says. "To shut you up, I'll go. I want to get off this goddamn island and get home. I'm freezing and hungry. Dustin, watch my back."

Dustin has already taken off his wet shirt and is preparing to jump in. Dustin waits for the right moment.

After taking a deep breath, Dustin dives in, swimming as fast as he can. The splash catches the predator's attention, causing it to circle back around. Dustin spots his attacker. With one swift kick on the nose, the shark turns away. Above the water, the others each have a hand in the water, splashing around. Running out of air, Dustin makes it to the desk. Ripping open the drawers, his eyes locate a yellow phone with a long antenna clipped to the side. As he turns to swim to the surface, the bull shark comes at him.

Full speed.

Everyone sees blood evaporate below. Jay shields Carly's eyes. John smacks the water. West is covering his mouth in shock. Suddenly, water splashes everywhere. "I got it!" Dustin yells as he frantically tries to escape the water. Jay and John quickly pull him up. Just in the nick of time, the shark's head popped out from beneath. Poor Dustin will have lost his donation center. Dustin flops on his back, huffing and puffing. West is relieved to see the sat phone held tightly to his chest. Dustin's partner checks him for any injuries. No blood appears on his hands.

"What happened?" John asks. "We thought it got you."

"No," Dustin says, still huffing. "He got close. I grabbed one of the dead guys and threw them in front of me."

"You fed a dead staff member of mine to a shark?" West asks, pissed off.

Dustin pushes himself up. "Look. I almost died for a fucking sat phone. A thank you would be really nice." Dustin smacks the phone into West's chest. While trying to get a signal, Dustin sits at the bar. He rewards himself with a beer.

For an hour, there is an unsuccessful attempt for a signal. After coming up with nothing, everyone decides to try and get some sleep. Some of the passengers lie on the sand, on big rocks. Though it is not the best place to sleep, everyone tries to get some shuteye.

Early the next morning, West and his crew attempt to bleed water from the ship. Hours later, they make some progress. The bull shark remains where they left it. As night falls, some passengers sleep on the island again. Jay, Carly, Dustin, and John decide to share a room together.

Late at night, the bitter cold air begins to turn warm. The wind that previously whipped through has died down. Carly is wrapped in Jay's arms—her little security blanket, she likes to think. Dustin and John make their chairs into uncomfortable beds. John tosses and turns. However, Dustin doesn't complain.

Carly suddenly awakens. She realizes that she needs to use the bathroom. Successfully, she frees herself from Jay's arms without waking him. Quietly, she walks past Dustin and John.

After finishing up in the bathroom, Carly walks back into the room. Her ear perches up. It comes from the hallway. Carly asks herself if she should wake Jay, but she disregards the idea. Carefully cracking the door open, she pokes her head out. Carly sees a little girl walking down the hallway, dragging a teddy bear behind her. "Mommy?" the child says, rubbing her eyes. Carly exits the room and walks over. "Mommy?" the child says it again.

"Hello?" Carly says. The little girl spins around; her face twists with fear. She holds her teddy bear close to her chest. Carly notices that the little girl looks as if she wants to cry. "Hi, sweetheart," Carly says, kneeling down. Carly eyes her up and down. The little girl has short brown hair and chubby cheeks. Carly guesses that she is at least eight years old.

"Hi," she says in a frightened tone. "I'm Ruby."

"Hi, Ruby. I'm Carly. What's wrong?"

"I can't find my mommy," Ruby says.

"Aww, I'm sorry, honey. What does she look like?"

"She um. Has um. Blonde hair, brown eyes. And an um, painting on her left ankle." Ruby clinches her teddy bear. Carly brushes her hair back behind her ear. "What's your mommy's name?"

"Donna," Ruby says. Tears pour from her eyes. "She told me she was going to the bathroom. I fell asleep, and then, then, when I woke up, she was gone."

Carly pushes Ruby's hair out of her face. "It's okay, honey. Your mommy will be back soon. Until then, do you wanna come stay with me, my husband, and his buddies? They'll protect you." Ruby shakes her head and follows Carly back to the room. Just as they get back, Jay is exiting the bathroom.

"You, okay? Who's this?" he asks.

"I'm Ruby."

"She couldn't find her mother," Carly says. "She can stay with us, right?"

Without a second thought, Jay says, "Put her in the bed. Make yourself comfortable, Ruby."

Carly and Ruby climb in bed with Jay. Out of nowhere was John's voice: "Hey, can I come cuddle too?"

Dustin, who didn't even open his eyes, says, "John. Go fuck yourself, then go back to sleep."

"Go fuck *yourself*," John replies.

"Mommy says don't say bad words," Ruby adds.

Carly can't help but smile at the bickering adults. Her smile goes away quickly. "Your mom's not here!" John says.

"John!" the three say simultaneously. Dustin gives John one good smack on the head with his bear claw. "What are you in the third fucking grade? Go to bed. Say that again, and I'll beat you into a coma!" Dustin says.

There was a long pause. Jay looks at Ruby. "Nice teddy bear."

"Thanks. His name is Peter."

CHAPTER 5

THE SUN CREATES A BEAUTIFUL painting. Dark clouds are taken over by a soon-to-be blue sky. Heat from the sun warms those who sleep on the sand. The tide moves closer and closer to the shore. Some unlucky sleepers get nailed with ice-cold water. Breakfast is brought out by the crew. The only thing ruining the view of the sunrise is the stranded *Wave Crusher*.

Rubbing her eyes, Carly turns over. She sees Ruby and her wonderful husband, who has given up most of the blanket to her. Carly shakes Jay's arm, startling him awake. "Good morning," Jay says, rubbing his eyes. While Dustin and John remain asleep, Ruby tells Jay what happened the night before. Jay and Carly agree that Ruby should stay with them until Donna comes back.

When Dustin and John are up and moving, they all take showers with barely warm, salty sea water. Thankfully, Jay and Carly have a waterproof suitcase. Unfortunately for John, he has to wear somewhat wet clothes. They are thankful their belongings are not swept away, unlike some passengers.

Searching for West, they find him in the employee break room. It is one of the few rooms barely damaged in the crash. A sign on the door reads EMPLOYEES ONLY. Dustin knocks. Seconds later, Jack appears on the other side. "Hey, guys. Come in." The group sits down at a small table. In the center is a bowl filled with candy bars and a few bottles of water; some are covered in dirt. The other side of the break room is a divider where there is a little lit room. Jay can hear a pencil writing on paper. He pokes his head around the corner to see West sitting at a once-full desk. While one hand holds his head up, the other takes notes. West spots Jay but says nothing.

"Didn't think I'd see you here," Jay says.

West never looks up. "I don't exactly have a room right now. So I'm sleeping in here for the time being."

Jay turns his attention to the table. John is eating one of the candy bars. Jack calls West from the other side. "Captain. What are we doing today?"

West huffs. "I don't know. I guess Donna didn't feel good last night. So she's probably not coming in."

Crickets.

Jack decides not to ask anything else.

Jay pulls up a chair. Shortly after, Jack and Dustin join them in the room.

While Jay and the guys are in the break room, Carly and Ruby play a game of tic-tac-toe on the bed. Ruby appears to be having fun. She smiles and occasionally laughs. As Ruby draws an X in one of the blocks, Carly takes a breath and asks, "Ruby, sweetheart? Can I ask you a question?" Ruby nods. Carly draws an O. "You talked about your mommy last night. What about your daddy?" Ruby pauses for a moment. Then she puts her pencil down and looks at the floor.

"I don't know much about my daddy," says Ruby. "When I talk about him to mommy, she cries. Then I'm sad because mommy's upset." Ruby picks her pencil up to draw another X. Again, Carly draws an O.

"Did your daddy…die?"

"I didn't go where you go when a person dies."

"A funeral?"

Ruby nods, then wins the game. Carly gives her a high five and gets a new piece of paper. Ruby draws four lines. "Do you know what your daddy looks like?"

"Kinda," Ruby says. "I'd have to see him."

Ruby draws an O.

"Miss Carly?"

"Yes?"

"I think my mommy said my daddy…left."

A chill crawls up Carly's spine. Her father left her and her mother at a young age. Carly could never find it in her heart to forgive him. When she was old enough to understand, Carly told her mother that she never wanted to see her father again. On one occasion, she ran into her father at the store. At first, she wasn't sure if the man was her dad. But many people have told her she looks a lot like him. As he walked over to her, Jay, who was only her boyfriend at the time, stepped in front of her. He told her dad to step off and stay away from her. After that, Carly's wish came true. She never saw him again. Years later, she learned that he committed suicide. Authorities said he went to a hotel room, took a bunch of pills, drank an entire bottle of liquor, closed his eyes, and never woke up. After his death, Carly honestly felt relieved. Neither she nor her mother attended the funeral. Since then, Carly's mother has remarried a kind and generous, hardworking man. Her mother always talks about how he takes care of her. Her mother has lived happily in Florida for the last ten years.

West has ordered Jack, Chad, and Cindy to attend to the passengers. Chad will cook, and Cindy will attend to those in need. Jay, Dustin, and John stay back to help West with the ship's repairs. Though the ship is not going anywhere, everyone knows that the water cannot keep coming in. As West and Dustin patch holes with pile wood, West keeps it in the storage room, and Jay and John pale water out of as many rooms as possible, except the control room.

West has one thing on his mind—the missing flare gun.

No one knows exactly where it is. For all West knows, it can be on the seafloor by now. Jay and John find a small jackpot while paling water—a large hunting knife, flares to the flare gun, wet pillows, unopened bottles of soda, keys, a speared bottle of wine, and two extra flashlights. Thankfully, they aren't toast from sitting in the water all this time.

West and Dustin finish up for the day. "Thanks for your help," West says. "Go tell the guys to get something to eat. It's on the house. I'm gonna see if I can make a call on the sat phone."

At dinner, Jay, John, and Dustin sit at the bar where Jay and Carly first came on the cruise. John waves his bottle, indicating it is empty. Chad, who is cleaning the bar with a damp rag, goes into the mini fridge and produces a fresh one. A few moments later, Cindy walks by. She grabs a napkin off the table, wiping her sweaty face with it. Chad says something to her, and she laughs. They kiss. Cindy enters the kitchen.

"Is that your lady friend?" John asks.

"Yes, she is," Chad says, ringing out the damp rag. "Met her on the job. She trained me. Been together for three years."

"Good for you," John says.

"What about you, guys?" Chad asks.

"Married, six years," Jay says.

"Single," says John.

Chad nods at Dustin. "What about you, bud?"

Dustin draws a long breath. "Widow."

Chad frowns. He wants to ask what happened but knows better. Chad turns on the ruined but somehow still working dishwasher. "I think God broke everything else except the shit we need to work." He grabs a rag to dry some glasses. Most of the glasses are broken from the crash. "Other than the current situation, how've you guys been?" Chad asks.

They all shoot the bull for a few minutes. Jay takes a big sip of beer. "Hey, Chad. Would you happen to know anything about a little girl named Ruby?"

Chad lifts his head from the fridge. "Donna's daughter? Yeah, I knew her since she was little. Why?"

"Was she the little girl who was with Carly this morning?" Dustin asks.

Jay nods. "Carly said she was walking alone last night. Said her mother left. But she never showed up. Hell, no one even looks or acts like they've lost a child."

"That's odd. Donna usually has a family member watch over her when she leaves home to come here," says Chad.

"Maybe she couldn't find a babysitter," John suggests.

As night falls, the guys head back to the room. Dustin remembers that West is trying to get a signal. He has not heard or seen him all night, so that probably means nothing. He and John go down the hall to take a leak. Jay gets back to the room, seeing that it is vacant. A note lies on the table. It reads, "*Jay, took Ruby outside for some air. If you get this, we'll be on the far side of the trees. See you soon! Love you!*"

Jay spots Carly and Ruby playing in the water. The sight gives Jay butterflies. For a while, they talk about having kids, but Jay isn't positive. Carly reaches down and picks up a small seashell. Ruby lights up with excitement. Jay can't help but smile. Carly sees her husband watching and waves. He presses his lips against hers, and they watch as Ruby plays in the water. Ruby sticks her hand in the water. What looks like a handful of sand turns out to be a starfish. "Look!" Ruby says with excitement. When the starfish is safely back in the water, Jay and Carly play with Ruby for a while longer.

Back in the room, John is drying off from a sea shower, and Dustin is reading a book he brought. It doesn't take long for any of them to fall asleep. Dustin, however, doesn't sleep much. Hours after everyone else is out for the night, he props his head up with his hand. Some nights, he fears falling asleep. He is afraid it will come back to him. The painful memory that haunts him to this day.

One of the most dreadful things that can happen, he has lived through. And he will continue to deal with it until God says his time is up.

CHAPTER 6

THE SHIP DOES NOT WAKE up early. Almost everyone decides to sleep in. The afternoon comes around. Passengers keep themselves occupied by swimming in the ocean, adventuring into the jungle, or climbing trees to get coconuts.

Inside the ship, the group wakes up one by one. Jay is the first to awaken. He goes into the bathroom, runs water over his face, then changes his shirt. Carly is awake. Jay gives her a kiss and slides back in bed. He grabs her butt and pulls her closer. "Dustin and John are right there," she whispers.

Jay considers. "Good point," he says. Jay gives his wife another kiss, his hand still on her butt. Dustin and John wake up and decide to stay in the room for a while longer. John complains of a headache. Dustin tells him not to drink so much. He goes back to his book, while everyone else does their own thing.

Night falls. Chad spends the night with Cindy. The couple holds hands, walking along the beach, the cold, wet sand underneath their toes. Waves continuously crash, and seagulls fly overhead. They talk about their first date, meeting each other's parents, and good times with friends.

"You know," Cindy says. "I haven't heard from Donna in a while. You think she still doesn't feel well?"

"Maybe. I saw her the other night. She looked like hell, to be honest."

"Should we go check on her?" Cindy asks. Chad nods. They go to the break room, grab the spare key, then head to Donna's room.

Coming down the hallway, Chad and Cindy find Donna's room. First, they knock. No answer. After waiting a moment, Chad knocks again. No answer. Cindy tries the doorknob.

Locked.

Pulling the key from his belt loop, Chad puts the key in the lock. "Donna?" he says. "It's Chad and Cindy. We're coming in." Turning the key and twisting the knob, Chad pushes the door open. It makes a little squeaking sound. The room is dark, and Chad has this feeling of bad energy.

Cindy looks at the corner of the room and covers her mouth, gasping, "Oh, my God!" she says. Chad sees what his lover sees. The scene steals the air from their lungs. "Go get help!" Cindy cries.

Jay and the guys sit in the room when suddenly Chad practically breaks the door down. Startled, they have trouble understanding what Chad is saying. When Chad catches his breath, he tells them.

Running as fast as lightning, John and Chad make it to the scene first. Dustin and Jay are right behind them. Though John has seen many scenes just like this one, the sight of the scene makes him nauseated.

Jay can't help but vomit in the hallway. Hanging from a beam, Donna swings back and forth. Her face is purple and puffy, and her eyes are swollen shut. A small stool stood underneath her. The rope makes a quiet, creaking sound.

John and Dustin carefully untie the noose and lay Donna's lifeless body on the bed. Taking a pencil and pulling the noose back from the neck, Dustin can see a dark, purple ring. It is the darkest black-and-blue mark he has ever seen. He realizes that the noose is tighter than usual. The rope almost cuts through the skin on her throat. If Donna committed suicide, she made sure the rope did the job. It is hard for Chad and Cindy to process this. Just the other day, Donna was sick. Now she's dead.

No one knows what to think.

Or what to do.

West stands alone in Donna's room. His heavy breathing can be heard. Frozen in shock, West stands as still as a statue. He then reaches out with his right hand, placing it on Donna's shoulder. "Rest," he whispers.

The noose remains around Donna's neck as they lay her down. West takes a pen from his pocket and writes on the door in bold letters—THIS ROOM IS OFF-LIMITS.

Clouds block the sun from shining. West orders not to say a word about yesterday. In his words, "Act as if it didn't happen." Is West hiding something? Anyone can be a suspect at this point.

Dustin and John take an early morning stroll. Their stroll goes into the forested area. Dustin picks up a rock and tosses it as they walk. "It had to have been a suicide," John says.

"How?" Dustin asks, tossing the rock. "We don't have evidence that Donna was depressed or anything."

This is why it is difficult for Dustin to work with John. He and Dustin can never agree on almost anything. And as partners, you have to agree on *some* things.

"John, I'm just saying. You and I searched the whole room last night. There wasn't even a note. Doesn't that send red flags?"

"Maybe she didn't feel the need to write one. We've seen that before. You've seen people do it for life insurance policies."

Dustin has not reply. Some people do not write a note. It can be possible. Dustin puts the idea on the back burner of his mind. Walking down the path, Dustin looks at John. John notices his partner giving him a funny look.

"Why are you lookin' at me like that?" John asks.

"Did you cut your cheek?"

"No, why?" John asks, confused.

"You have blood on your face."

John wipes his cheek with the back of his hand. Smeared blood appears. He has felt something run down his cheek. He just assumes it is just sweat, considering it is hot today. They look up. Nothing is there, just leaves mixed with branches. Dustin sticks out his hand. A tiny drop of blood splatters on his palm. Looking at the ground, they notice a small pool of blood at their feet.

Climbing the trees, John and Dustin attempt to locate the source of the mysterious blood. Reaching the top, they begin pulling away at the leaves and tangled vines. With one final tug, their hearts drop to their stomachs. Hanging by her feet, a woman dangles from the branches with vines tied around her ankles. Her face is purple, her eyes bulge, dark circles form under her eyes, her throat is cut from ear to ear, and blood is oozing. Flies fly in and out of the woman's slit throat, mouth, and nose. The odor of the decaying body rises into the air. It makes both Dustin and John gag and nearly vomit. It is difficult for them not to look into her eyes—her innocent eyes. Her body slowly turns in a circle. The blood oozing from her throat runs down her face and into her hair. The unknown woman's ankles are purple, like Donna's neck.

John and Dustin climb down. They look as if they have seen a ghost. Pale and nauseated, they try to find words. Dustin sits on the ground, raking his hair back. John moves a few feet away behind a tree, trying not to lose his lunch. Dustin covers his ears, toning out the terrible sounds coming from John. John comes back with some color restored to his face.

"Let's talk," John finally says.

CHAPTER 7

MEANWHILE, CHAOS RISES BACK AT the ship. The word about Donna's body spreads like a bad rash. West attempts to calm everyone down and assures them that nothing is wrong and the story is not true. If only it wasn't true. Jay and Carly watch over Ruby, but no one has said, "That's my daughter." Carly pulls Jay to the side.

"Jay, I don't know what to do. Dustin tells me Donna possibly didn't commit suicide. I'm really scared."

"I know," Jay says, touching her shoulder. "But as long as you have three guys with you, you'll be safe."

Looking over Jay's shoulder, Carly sees Dustin, along with John, emerging from the trees. Both look tired, pale, and traumatized. Dustin tells them what they saw. Jay and Carly stand in silence. John spots West by the water, rinsing his hands. He walks over and taps him on the shoulder. John whispers in his ear. West frowns. He then places his hat on his head and begins to walk away. John beckons his hand.

Follow the leader.

They follow West to the break room. His head rests in his hand, and his face holds disappointment. "Where did you find her?" West asks.

"Hanging by her feet in the trees," John says in a deep voice.

West stands up and looks at everyone. "Alright. Here's what we're gonna do. We'll go cut her down and bring her back to the room across from Donna. I'll lock it up. Tomorrow, we're gonna find that fucking flare gun and shoot that motherfucker when a plane flies

33

by. If that doesn't work, I'll do everything I can to get the sat phone working. Sound good?"

Everyone agrees. West reaches into his boot and produces the large hunting knife found earlier. He hands it to John, who tucks it in his waist belt.

A few minutes later, Dustin and John go back into the trees. John puts the blade between his teeth and begins his climb. When the vines are cut, the partners carefully lower her to the ground.

Making sure the coast is clear, Dustin and John pull the body back to the ship. Finally, they make it back without getting any unwanted attention. When everything is complete, Dustin locks the door behind him.

Night falls. A chill rolls in the air. Since some extra blankets are washed away in the sea, the passengers use towels, extra clothes, or anything they can find to stay warm. Jay is sound asleep when he is awakened by a shaking bed. Carly is dreaming again. She grips the sides of the bed and screams in a low tone. Her forehead is layered with sweat, and then she starts throwing punches. Jay tries to wake her. Carly wakes up, nearly screaming. Running into the bathroom, she throws water in her face. Their roommates are awakened by the sounds of her heavy breathing.

"You okay?" Jay asks.

"Another nightmare."

"Must have been a pretty bad one," Dustin says. "What happened?"

"I…I don't know. It was blurry."

"That happened the last time," Jay says.

"She may just be paranoid," John adds.

After Carly is calmed down, they walk her back to bed. She is soon fast asleep when her head hits the pillow. Jay, John, and Dustin stay awake. They sit outside in the hallway. John looks at his watch. It's currently two thirty in the morning. He huffs as he throws his head against the wall. Dark circles form under their eyes, and they yawn uncontrollably.

"Jay?" says John. "Did you say Carly had dreams like this before?"

Jay tiredly shakes his head as he yawns. "Yeah, she had one the night we got her. She said the dreams were blurry. I don't understand that."

"I'm not sure about that either," Dustin says. "She's probably scared of the situation. But if you said it happened the night before, then I don't know. Maybe her mind is trying to tell her something. She just can't figure it out."

Jay shrugs. They stay where they are until the sun rises. None of them knows why Carly is having these dreams.

West looks out into the sea. His mind is like its waves, constantly moving. His mind travels back to the missing flare gun. Whether they are gonna get rescued. Suddenly, Jack comes in the door. His face is sweaty, looking as tired as a dog.

"We have a problem," he says.

CHAPTER 8

THE GANG GATHERS IN THE break room. West's hands hold his head up. He huffs with frustration and aggravation. His usually clean uniform is worn raggedly, his hair a mess, and his eyes dark. Jack leans against the wall, hands behind his back, and head resting on the wall. Dustin and John sit in the middle of the room, nearly falling asleep. Jay and Carly stand by a broken window.

"You wanna tell us why you called us here, *captain*?" Dustin asks, rubbing his chin.

"Sure thing, *Dustin*," West says sarcastically. "I'd be very happy to tell you. Not only can I not get a signal on the satellite phone, I was just informed that we're running out of food."

Dustin jumps out of his chair. The tone of his voice changes.

"Satellite phone? Really? You seem more worried about that phone than you do about getting off the island. What kind of a captain are you?"

"Okay. First, don't be an asshole 'cause you think you're better than me. Second, I want to go home too. But in order to do so, I need the phone. No phone, no going home."

"I agree!" Dustin shouts. "But we have been stranded in the middle of fucking nowhere for over a week! And after doing some thinking, I don't think Donna killed herself. I think there's a fucking killer onboard. You wanna get your head cut off? You know what? Since you keep delaying getting off the ship, I think *you* may be the killer!"

West's face turns red with anger. He and Dustin continue to go at it. The rest of the gang sits and listens. Jay, who was getting frustrated himself, sits at the table, burying his head. West and Dustin continue to spit insults at each other. Jay picks his head up. Carly sees her husband's anger. A fire builds up in his belly. A short dynamite fuse is lit inside him. Finally, he has enough. He fills his lungs with as much air as possible.

With closed fists, he rises from his seat and pounds on the table. "Heeeyyy!" he cries. "Both of you sit your asses in those chairs! I swear to God, if you move, I'll beat the goddamn life from you! There has been a lot of arguing, and no work is getting done! And being children will not get us anywhere!"

West and Dustin *sit their asses down*. Jay fixes his shirt as he stands and walks to the corner of the room. Everyone stares at him in shock. Carly keeps her distance. Her body shakes from shock and fear.

Once the tension in the air decreases, the conversation starts up again. The topic is what they can do for food, water, and everything else they need to survive. "What about the shark in the control room?" asks Jay, still red-faced.

"What about it?" John asks.

"Is it still there?"

"There's a chance it could be," West says.

Jay takes the hunting blade from West, which is tucked in his boot. He twists it in his hand as if it were the most beautiful thing he has ever seen. "Who wants to go fishing?"

There it is, circling the floor of the control room. Two dead bodies remain strapped to chairs. One is badly chewed from the previous attack. Bones show, flesh hangs off, parts of the skull are exposed, and the right eye is gone. The arms are torn to bits, the chest is ripped open, and the fingers are missing.

Butterflies rise in their stomachs. In the last encounter, Dustin almost died. If it weren't for the bodies, Dustin would probably be dead or seriously hurt. They stand over the predator, waiting for the right moment.

Jay pokes his index finger with the knife and squeezes. Little droplets of blood fall into the water. The shark swims to the surface. Jay drives the knife down behind the dorsal fin. John and Dustin heave the shark to the floor. Repeatedly jabbing the knife in the back, Jay creates ten stab wounds. When the moment stops, Jay slides the blade down its belly. Digging in, Jay sees an orange object. "Captain," Jay says, tossing it. West fumbles the object.

It was the flare gun.

"Now go see if you can find the flares."

West notices the flare gun is covered in blood and something else. "Where in the shark did you find this?"

"In its anus," Jay says.

West looks at the gun with disgust.

CHAPTER 9

THE SUN PEAKS OVER THE horizon, terminating the cold air with a warm breeze. As the group sleeps soundly, Ruby wakes up. She realizes that she is the only one awake this morning. Ruby sees that Peter is not with her, and she gets out of bed to look for him. Not seeing him on the bed or floor, Ruby focuses her attention underneath the bed. There is nothing but total darkness. Ruby slowly kneels down, waiting for something to jump out at her. Ruby is relieved to see Peter, not a monster. However, something else catches her eye. Something shiny.

A key.

Ruby grabs the key in her hand. Making sure she doesn't wake anyone, she walks over to the door. Carefully turning the knob, Ruby opens the door. She holds Peter in one hand and the key in the other. Her little heart pounds, hoping she won't get caught.

Standing in the hallway, with not another soul in sight, Ruby sees a door just a few feet from their room. If she is reading it correctly, it reads: THIS ROOM IS OFF-LIMITS. Ruby puts the key in the lock. The room is as dark as a cave. Butterflies erupt in her belly. Taking a big breath and swallowing her fear, Ruby takes a step into the room, leaving the key in the lock. Walking farther into the room, Ruby covers her mouth with her free hand. Ruby's foot catches something, making her fall. Grabbing her elbow in pain, Ruby looks around as best she can. It is almost impossible to see anything with the naked eye.

Ruby feels around for Peter on the floor. Suddenly, she feels what she thinks is a large sheet. Thanks to the dim light coming from the light in the hallway, Ruby is able to confirm that it is a sheet. Lifting the sheet, fear waved over her. A human foot. Not knowing any better, Ruby grabs the ankle and turns it. She sees a *painting* that looks familiar. The *painting* is a white rose with the word "Daddy" written along the vine. Crawling to the top of the sheet, Ruby slowly pulls, and what she sees horrifies her. Her heart stops, and she begins to feel lightheaded. "Mommy?" she says. "Mommy! Mommy, wake up!"

Ruby grabs Peter and runs out of the room, tears streaming down her face. She sits outside the open door, crying into her arms. Even though she is only eight years old, Ruby knows that her mommy is never going to wake up.

The sound of a whimpering child opens Jay's eyelids. Jumping out of bed, he finds Ruby in the hallway. "Ruby, what's wrong?" As he kneels down, Jay realizes that the forbidden door is open. That is when he dashes over to close it. He knows what she has been crying about. Jay feels a wave of sadness.

Soon after, the rest gathered around. When Ruby is calmed down, they take her back to their room. Carly puts her in bed and tells her that everything is okay, although they all know that every-thing is not okay. Ruby, a young child, just discovered the horrible thing that happened to her mother.

A few hours go by. Jay, John, and Dustin cram in the bathroom to talk.

"What are we supposed to do?" Dustin asks.

"I don't know," Jay yells in a whisper. "You're the expert with this. What do you suggest?"

Silence. Then it hits Jay.

"Wait a minute, Dustin? Where did you hide the key?"

"I gave it to John."

"And I put it under the bed," says John.

Both Jay and Dustin glare at him, almost with disgust. "How was I supposed to know she would look there? Most kids her age hate looking under the bed. You know what I'm talking about. As kids, we all hated that."

The men talk a while longer. By the time they were done, it was late afternoon. Jay and Dustin go for a walk. Carly and Ruby go out to the water. John stays where he is. Thinking about how a little mistake he made has caused a child horrific trauma.

Carly and Ruby sit in the sand, feet buried and water cooling their toes. Carly asks Ruby about her mother. What she was like and what she liked to do. Little questions. Ruby teaches Carly another thing. The tattoo on Donna's ankle is for her father. He died of a heart attack just five years ago. For a while longer, they sit on the beach.

CHAPTER 10

DUSTIN ENTERS THE FORBIDDEN ROOM when the smell hits him in the face, burning his nostrils. Trying to not be bothered by it, Dustin closes the door, turns on the light, and walks over to Donna. Pulling off the sheets, Dustin leans in close to examine. Unable to help it, the smell from Donna's body makes him gag. The purple mark left behind by the rope created a new haunting memory. He played the scene through his head. There was no note and nothing to prove that Donna wanted to end her life. It could have been a last-minute situation, but Dustin thought it was unlikely. Until they get off the island, Dustin can only suspect a killer. Only he has no idea who it can be.

Dustin notices something—a red ring on Donna's left ring finger. He takes a mental note of it. He moves on to Jane Doe's room. He looks down at her throat. The tissue and muscles are visible. If the cut had been any deeper, Jane Doe's head would have fallen off. Dustin knows this could not have been self-harm. She would have bled out by the time she cut her throat completely. Plus, there is no knife where she is found. And the area looks undisturbed.

The thought comes to Dustin. Can this mystery woman kill Donna, then herself? John walks into the room, catching him by surprise. Dustin decides to wrap it up.

"What are you doing?" John asks.

"What does it look like I'm doing?"

"It looks like you're not listening. The bodies shouldn't be touched until we get back home."

"When do you know we're going home?" Dustin says, getting irritated. "John, are you forgetting that we've been stuck here for over a week? No one has come to look for us. For Christ's sake, there are dead bodies on the ship, and there's a killer right next to us."

"Dustin," John says. "These women committed suicide."

"God damn it! You don't know that! You and I have seen multiple suicides. These two are missing all kinds of pieces to the puzzle. As far as we know, Donna and this woman had no reason to die like this. And I'm sorry if you don't agree with me, but damn it, John, you don't listen to anybody."

Dustin walks out before John can say anything.

Carly rests in a deep sleep. Suddenly, she sits up in bed. She walks into the hallway. It has a dark and eerie look and feel to it. Lights flicker on and off; a very human chill runs up your spine; whispers echo behind closed doors. Carly is the only one awake. She can't put her finger on why she's up walking around. Maybe she's sleepwalking. She takes small steps down the hall. "Caaarrlly," a voice whispers. Carly turns around.

No one.

Carly turns in the other direction. "Caaarrlly."

No one.

Carly walks in the direction of the voice. There is nothing but darkness. The darkness closed in on her. "Carly. Come closer," the voice urges.

"Hello?" Carly whispers.

A person's face peaks from the darkness. Carly stumbles as she falls to the ground. She closes her eyes, hoping that what she is seeing will go away. It does not. Carly's throat feels as if it swells shut. The face comes out further from the shadows.

It is Donna.

"What do you want?" Carly asks.

Donna puts her index finger up to her mouth. "Shhhhhh," she says. Donna then runs her hand across her purple neck, whispering something.

"What?" Carly asks again.

"Shhhh," says Donna.

Donna then holds her left hand out. Carly sees a red ring around her ring finger. She beckons Carly to come closer. Carly hesitates. Finally, she leans in, sticking out her ear. In a low, hoarse voice, Donna whispers, "Find him."

Carly pulls away, confused. "What?"

"Find him."

"Who's him?"

"FIND HIM!"

Donna vanishes back into the dark hallway. Carly sits there, afraid to move. Dragging her butt across the floor, she shuffles herself against the wall, scaring herself. She begins to weep quietly. Tears burn her cheeks.

Carly is startled when a hand lands on her shoulder. It is Jay. "Carly? What's wrong, love?" he kneels down, rubbing her arms, causing her to look up.

"I…I…something woke me up. I got up and…and," she stutters between huffs and cries. Jay hushes her soothingly, hugging her.

"Why are you crying, love?" he asks her softly.

"Donna…told me to 'find him.' But I don't know what that means. And she came from nowhere. I don't know why she did that to me."

Jay looks at her, confused.

"Jay, I'm really scared. I don't want anything to happen to me. I don't want to find whoever she's talking about."

Jay hushes her soothingly again and strokes her hair. "It's okay. We'll figure it out. I'm sure it's nothing. Come on, let's go back to bed."

CHAPTER 11

RAIN POURS FROM THE SKY. Sand becomes heavy, and leaves spill water like a waterfall. Waves smack against the side of the ship, causing it to rock and causing more damage to the side. Lighting strikes through the sky. The group is huddled in the room, protecting themselves from any possible debris. Ruby tucks under a desk, holding Peter close to her. Jay manages to find his gun in his suitcase. Making sure it's tucked safely in his waistband, Jay wraps his arms around Carly, holding her tight.

West stands outside, braving the storm. Dripping wet from head to toe, West looks up into the dark sky. As the rain soaks into his face, he hears a loud beeping—the sat phone. He removes it from his belt.

"Hello!" he yells.

"This is the United States Coast Guard! Who am I speaking with?"

"My name is Captain Alvin West! I need assistance at the following coordinates!" West spits them into the phone. "I say again, we need immediate assistance! Our ship has crashed, and we've been stranded!"

Total madness occurs inside the ship. Lights flicker on and off, water runs through the hall, and random objects float around. Everyone is terrified of not making it through this. They are able to make it despite the ship crashing, but they don't know what to expect now.

Anything can happen.

The storm starts letting up. As the rain drifts away, the group is surprised by a visit from West. He stands in the doorway, completely soaked. They know he has something to say. All of them hope it is something good.

"Can anyone build a raft?"

Though rain lightly falls, everyone in the group helps build rafts. The bottom is made of layers of tree logs. The sail is made from a few pipes and a shower curtain. When the job is almost complete, John decides to have a quick conversation with West.

"Captain?" he says.

"Yes, John?"

"What are we going to do about the others?"

West hesitates. "Well...I was thinking."

"About?"

West hesitates again.

"Wait. So all of us are just gonna abandon the passengers?"

West removes his hat. "I wouldn't say abandoned. We just leave for a while. It's not like I won't send help back."

John isn't sure about what to think or say. Why would the captain of a ship just get up and leave his passengers? Even though thoughts run through his mind, John doesn't want to argue. It is the last thing they need.

Just before everyone departs on the raft, Carly goes to use the bathroom. She notices that Dustin has wandered off earlier and hasn't returned. On her way back to her husband, Carly is surprised to spot Dustin. She sees him sitting at the edge of the water by one end of the trees, tucked away from everyone else. Carly approaches.

"Hey, Dustin," she says. "We're gonna head out soon."

"Okay," Dustin says, nodding. "I'll only be a minute."

"Whatcha got there?" Carly asks.

Without looking, Dustin speaks quietly. "My wife's necklace. I held on to it after she...you know."

"May I sit?"

Dustin extends his hand. "Of course."

Carly knows that she is not in the right place. But from the first day she and Dustin met, she knew he might have lied about

ALL HANDS ON DEATH

his wife. If it hadn't been for John, Carly would not be having this conversation.

"Dustin?" she says. "Forgive me if I'm out of line. But I have something to ask."

Dustin slightly frowns. "What is it?"

"How…I know…your wife."

"How did my wife die?" Dustin finishes. He doesn't need Carly to say yes. His wife's death is always a secret he keeps to himself. It's not a subject he likes, just like anyone else who lost a lover.

"Yeah," Carly says shyly.

Dustin's eyes waters. Carly can hear him breathing the way you do when you fight back tears. His focus is on the necklace. Dustin clears his throat. "You know, I don't really like to talk about it."

"Okay, I'm sorry," Carly says.

"She died right in front of me," Dustin says as Carly goes to stand. "I held her in my arms. There wasn't much I could do."

"I'm really sorry."

"I always say…" Dustin again clears his throat. "It was breast cancer, because then I can try to escape what really happened to her."

Carly doesn't say a word. *What do I say?* she thinks. Finally, she finds the courage.

"What happened to her?"

Los Angeles. Night has fallen as humidity hangs in the air. The streets are quiet and calm. A few officers roam the streets, keeping an eye on crime. Officer Dustin King of the Los Angeles Police Department Headquarters is one of the few roaming the streets. It is approaching 9:30 p.m. So far, everything is going smoothly.

Driving down the street, Dustin sees another set of headlights. Suddenly, the driver flashes their lights at him. Gently stepping on the brake, Dustin completely stops in the middle of the road. The driver rolls down the window, and Dustin smiles at who he sees. The driver is his wife, Melanie. "Hey, stranger," she says.

"How's it going, pretty lady?"

"Other than a few traffic stops, it's pretty slow."

"Same. I mean, if you want, we can go in the trees there, and…"
Dustin revs his Charger's engine while raising his eyebrows.

Melaine looks at her husband. "I don't think so, mister."

Just then, a call comes over the scanner. "All units, 10-16 in progress on Pine Oak Street. The suspect is considered dangerous and under the influence."

Dustin and Melaine exchange looks. "You wanna go for it?" Melaine asks.

"967 responding," Dustin says into his radio.

"824 responding as backup."

Together, Dustin and Melaine meet in the academy and fall in love. When they join the force, Dustin knows that they both will not be able to work at the same station. So, in order for both their dreams to come true, Dustin takes a job at the LA Headquarters, then Melanie at Hollenbeck.

Their love for each other is no secret. Their chiefs are fully aware. Unless absolutely necessary, both Dustin and Melanie are instructed not to interact with each other on the clock.

But on this night, all of that is about to change.

Dustin and Melaine arrive at the address, lights and sirens off. Before approaching the front door, the couple notice a few odd things. The lights are off. Nothing seems to be disturbed. Dustin keeps a hand on the handle of his gun. They approach.

Dustin knocks. "LAPD!" he calls out. There is no answer. "LAPD!" Dustin says it again. At that moment, Melaine swears she heard a man clear his throat. Something doesn't feel right. A call is made here, but no one is responding. Maybe it is a homicide now. Both of them have seen many things happen like that.

"We should go in," says Dustin.

"I don't know, Dust. I've got a bad feeling."

"Look, if we go in and everything's good, we'll leave. How's that?"

Melaine only nods. To their surprise, the door is unlocked. With the lights off, you can't see your hand in front of your face. Using their flashlights, they carefully scope the place. "Split up," Dustin whispers. Melaine takes the right, and Dustin takes the left.

The house is a lot bigger than they think. The trash covers most of the floor. Dustin manages to stay quiet with firearms aimed and light guiding. His ears only catch the sound of his pounding heart. Right in front of him is a door. Dustin twists the knob, walking out of sight.

Melaine walks quietly upstairs. Little noises all around her make her jump. Her usually steady hand becomes shaky. She finds herself at the top of the steps. At the end of the hallway, Melaine sees a door standing ajar. A dim light exposes the outline of the wooden door. Ignoring her thoughts, Melaine walks closer. Taking a breath, she pushes the door open with her foot. Melaine is surprised by a shadowed figure sitting at a small round table. The shadow is playing cards. "Police!" Melaine yells. "Let me see your hands!" The shadow doesn't seem shocked. "Hands now!" Melaine yells again. The shadow looks at her with colorless eyes.

"You've been betrayed, Melaine," the shadow says in a deep voice.

Melaine lowers her weapon the slightest. "You know my name?" She knows she should not have asked that question. The shadow slowly lifts its hand. "Don't move!" Melaine cries. The shadow pulls down its hood. Melaine sees that *it* is a *he*.

"I know who you are," Melaine says, her voice shaken.

Dustin scours the basement. Shots ring out upstairs, echoing in Dustin's ears. "Dustin!" Melaine cries into her radio. Dustin reaches for his radio and says, "967, shots fired! Shots fired! Officer in trouble!" Doing a 360-degree spin, Dustin runs back up the stairs. To his discovery, it has been locked from the other side.

"Shit!" he yells. Dustin tries kicking the door down. Boom! It doesn't budge. Again, boom! Still not moving. He puts everything he has on this kick. Boom! There is a loud thud on the other side. He sees the knob completely come off as the door opens, enough for him to get out. Dustin is surprised to see a black, shadowy figure on the ground. Quicker than the blink of an eye, the figure fishes a shiny object from their pocket and points at Dustin. Without thinking, Dustin discharges his firearm four times. A sharp pain rips through his shoulder. He has been shot. Gripping his wound and standing over the figure, Dustin sees a young, white male, probably no older than twenty-one, bleeding out; there is no life left in him. A chair with a broken leg now lies in the way of the door. Dustin realizes that the door has not been *locked* but *blocked*. He has to get to Melaine.

Running down the hallway, Dustin still can't find Melaine. She keeps screaming, "Dustin!" into her radio. More shots are fired. "Melaine!" No answer. "Melaine!" He presses the button on his radio. "Melaine, where are you?" Over the radio, Melaine came, almost out of breath.

"I'm outside, behind my cruiser!" Dustin runs out the door. Right out front of the house, gunfire echoes. Melaine ducks behind her cruiser. He fires his weapon while making his way to her.

"Are you hit?" he asks.

"No," Melaine says. "What do we do?"

Dustin scopes the area. A few feet away is a concrete wall in someone's yard. "Move over there for better cover! Be careful!"

"Don't worry," Melaine says. "We're gonna get the upper hand, and we're gonna kill them all." Melaine looks over her cruiser, checking if she has a clear shot at running for the concrete wall. "Moving!"

Melaine positions herself behind the wall. There are five armed suspects. Lights in houses turn on as citizens are awoken. Dustin orders bystanders to get back inside. Backup has to be on its way. "Dispatch! I need that backup *now*!" Dustin screams into his radio.

Reloading, the sound of sirens comes screaming down the road. Screeching to a halt, another officer gets out of the car. "John!" Dustin cries.

"You good?" John yells over the gunfire. A bullet strikes the top of the cruiser.

"I got five suspects heavily armed! Three that way, and two over there! I think we can take 'em, but we need more firepower!"

"Roger that!" John yells. Ducking his way to his cruiser, he comes back with a shotgun. One of the suspects makes a run for it.

"Mel!" John yells. "After him!"

"Mel, wait!" Dustin yells. Melaine is already running through a row of houses. The gunfire only elevates. Dustin becomes more worried about his wife. He looks for John, who ducks on the other side of the car, avoiding bullets.

"John!" Dustin puts a new mag in his sidearm. "On three, you're gonna empty your gun and light these motherfuckers up!" Dustin pauses. "One, two, three!"

Shotgun shells escape the chamber. Three of them hit the suspects; one successfully makes it out and runs. Both officers chase after him. John reloads as he runs. "LAPD! Stop!" John orders.

Gunshots echo down an alleyway. There is a scream. "Melaine!" Dustin yells.

"Go!" John yells. "I got him. Go!"

Dustin peels away from John as he runs to find his wife. So much went through his head. What happened? Who was shot? Melaine doesn't radio for help.

Running toward the alley, Dustin spots a tall figure standing over a person. He is standing over Melaine, kicking her. "Hey!" Dustin cries. Lifting his weapon, Dustin pulls the trigger twice. The bullets hit the figure. The figure runs off, not fazed at all, it seems.

Dustin runs over to Melaine.

"Mel!" he yells. Her uniform is caked with blood. Dustin checks for a pulse. Thank God she has one. Pressing his hand on her wound, Melaine lets out a quiet moan. She attempts to push his hand away. "Melaine, stop moving. I need to put pressure on your wound!"

Melaine gives off faint breaths. Blood slowly leaks from her chest. Dustin keeps his focus on his wife, only looking up when he hears a noise. With his other hand, Dustin snatches his radio. "967! Officer down! Officer down! I need paramedics! Officer down in the alleyway on Fourth Street! 10–3!"

"All units, all LA units, officer down! 4th Street alleyway. All available units respond," dispatch repeats.

Dustin puts his forehead to Melaine's, sobbing. Melaine grips his wrist, giving Dustin all the hope he needs.

"Stay with me, Melaine! Please don't leave me!"

Melaine pulls her husband closer, crying on his shoulder. "I love you, Dustin!" she says. "I love you so much."

"Melaine," Dustin says, crying. "Save your strength."

"I'm gonna be okay," Melaine says. "You're my strength."

Dustin becomes speechless. Melaine's love makes sure she continues to breathe. So far, she has kept herself alive.

Dustin shouts into his radio. "OFFICER DOWN, I NEED SOME HELP! PLEASE I NEED SOME FUCKING HELP! WHERE THE FUCK IS THE CALVARY!" The cry vibrates his lungs, shaking with anger and anxiety.

"Dustin?" Melaine whispers. "Wh...white male. Shaved head... Tat...Tat...tattoo...arm, arm."

"What color tattoo?"

"Bl-blue, large...creature. Red-colored creature."

White male, shaved head, blue tattoo, large red-colored creature. Dustin drills the description into his memory.

"I love you, Dustin," Melaine whispers, rubbing her husband's smooth, sweaty cheek.

"I love you too, Melaine," Dustin says, smiling at his wife.

Melaine's eyes close as she slumps in Dustin's arms. "Melaine?" Tears drip down Dustin's cheeks. "Melaine? Melaine, please wake up." Sobs fill the air. "Melaine, come back...come back."

"After she died, I took this off her." Dustin dangles a chain wrapped around his fingers, showing Carly the necklace. It is a cross with a purple birthstone in the center and *Melaine* on the back, written in cursive. Dustin has carried it with him since Melaine's passing. "I know I should have kept it on her, but I didn't want to take her wedding band."

"I'm so sorry, Dustin," Carly says.

"Thank you... I miss her a lot."

"How have you been since?"

Dustin lets out a quiet sigh. "Okay, I guess. After the chief found out, he called me into his office. The group that we took down was a gang named the California Killers. Mel is a part of an operation that arrested the leader of the group. I got suspended and assigned a new partner. You know, to *keep an eye on me.* That's why John is here."

"But, Dustin. Had you not gone with your wife, you wouldn't have been able to say goodbye. It wasn't the way you wanted, but she saw you before she...passed."

"My chief didn't care. He was sympathetic, but he didn't act that way."

Carly waves her hand. "Ah, fuck him. Losing a loved one is hard."

Dustin nods.

"What happened to the guy John was chasing?" Carly asks.

Melaine is taken to the morgue. Dustin and John stand behind the one-way glass in the interrogation room. John apprehends the suspect, then brings him back to the headquarters. Now it was the detective's turn to try and get this guy to talk.

The suspect was a thirty-year-old drug addict. He has filthy-looking skin, a rough beard, and a shaved head. The detective investigating the case enters the room with her proper essentials. She sits down and begins.

"Sir, you heard your rights, and now this is your chance to help us out here. Do you have anything to say? Or anything you want to tell me?"

"I'm not talking until I have a lawyer," the shaved head says.

Dustin, who still has his wife's dry blood on his hands, feels his rage boil inside him. He taps John on the shoulder. "Give me that keycard."

John does so.

"If you have noth—" beep.

The door opens. Dustin stands face-to-face with the shaved head. He turns to the detective.

"Go and get a coffee. I'll take it from here."

The detective exits the room.

Dustin yanks the chair out and sits down, looking at the shaved head in the eye the entire time. "You want to tell me who your friend was? Meaning the one who ran into the alleyway."

"I got nothing to say. I want a lawyer."

"Yeah, I heard you," Dustin snaps. "You won't walk out of this room until you tell me who your buddy is."

"Lawyer," the shaved head repeated.

Dustin brings his fists down hard on the table. "Do you see the blood on my hands! I've got my wife's blood on them! And if you don't tell me who killed her, you're gonna be sorry!"

The shaved head only sits and stares. He adjusts his cuffed wrists. He then leans in, and Dustin can smell his sweat.

"I can't tell you without my lawyer," the shaved head whispers.

Dustin snatches the shaved head by the collar of his shirt. "Yes, you can!" he cries. In one swift motion, Dustin lifts him out of his chair, throwing him up against the one-way glass, causing it to crack. "Yes, you can!" Dustin yells.

John rushes into the room with the detective. John wraps his arms around Dustin. Eventually, they pry him off, taking the shaved head to another room. Dustin is told by his chief that he is lucky not to be fired. Now that Melaine is gone, Dustin is justified.

Jay comes looking for Carly and tells them that it is time to go. This is the moment of truth. West and the gang are gonna leave the rest of the passengers behind and bring back help. It is risky, but something has to be done.

Rain falls hard on the makeshift raft. The once-blue water appears to turn black as waves crash into the boat. John and Dustin pale out the water with their bare hands. Carly holds onto Ruby, and Jay holds onto Carly.

West does his best to keep the raft straight, moving the bedsheet sail in the direction of the wind. Everyone is soaked from head to toe and getting pelted by the rain. Some people say that when it rains, it means God is angry. The good Lord certainly is upset today.

Though the water is no longer clear, John is positive that he sees a shark...or two.

Not little ones like before.

Possibly Great Whites.

Though the vision in the sky is dark like the water, as West guides the sail, his eye catches something—a red dot and a blinking white dot.

Helicopter?

"Jay," West cries over the pounding rain. "Toss Me The Flare Gun!"

Jay pulls the orange gun from his waistband. West one hand snatches it. With his other hand, West pulls the hammer back with his thumb. Raising his arm high above his head, West fires the flare. A red trail follows the little ball of red fire.

The flare disappears into the black clouds.

Nothing appears to happen.

West tosses the gun back to Jay, who reloads it. West repeats his action.

A heavy gust of wind comes over them, nearly tipping the hand-crafted raft tip over. A large, red-colored chopper emerges from the clouds.

West laughs with excitement.

The Coast Guard on the side of a chopper is approaching their faces. The pilots hover above them, throwing a ladder down the side. *Bang!* Something zips past them. *Bang!* Everyone on the raft looks around. What can be coming at them?

Bang!

This one whizzes past Dustin's head. A Coast Guard member screams down the ladder. "Climb up! Hurry!"

Bang!

This time, it zips past John. Bullets from the chopper's FN M240H spit in the direction of the boat. "Woah, woah!" West yells at the pilot. "There are passengers on that ship!"

"We're being shot at, Captain! It's a risk that needs to be taken!" The pilot turns to the gunner. "Keep firing!" The gunner does as he was told. Jay helps Carly get her balance on the out-of-control ladder. Jay then carries Ruby on his shoulders while he climbs.

Bang! Bang!

A bullet strikes the side of the chopper. The gunner is showing no mercy or fear. Dustin and John are the last to climb aboard the chopper, still trying to avoid being struck by the flying bullets. The pilot whisks them away from the scene. The gang's makeshift raft flips over in the sea. The gunner is standing his ground. "Cease-fire! Cease-fire!" The FN M240H's barrel steams from the cold rain wind.

"Nice shooting," Jay says. The gunner nods at Jay.

Captain West informs the pilot of the remaining passengers. The Coast Guard pilot sends more rescue teams. Hours later, everyone is saved. West mentions the dead bodies. He tells them, "Be careful, men. Contaminate those bodies, and you'll mess up the whole case."

Later, when autopsies are performed, Jane Doe is identified as Jenna Quiver. Something about that name gives Dustin a funny feeling. Putting his thoughts to the side, Dustin joins the others. Happy to be heading home.

CHAPTER 12

A FEW WEEKS HAVE PASSED since the rescue. Donna's and Jenna Quiver's bodies are laid to rest. Both are buried at the local cemetery. Paparazzi and the news cover the story, asking members of the group to do interviews. It is said that the *Wave Crusher* remains where it crashed, but it eventually sinks due to the amount of rain and water, causing it to take on weight and slide into the open water. So much for attempting to collect any evidence for the bodies.

Even with all the interviews and annoying questions, most of the survivors try to go back to their normal lives. Jay and Carly pack up and move to Delaware, hoping for a fresh start and no cameras pointing at them while they are in public. Jay finds a new accounting firm to work at. Carly does her wedding planning. Ruby's aunt takes custody of her when she discovers that her niece is still alive.

Back in Los Angeles, Dustin and John continue their work on the force. This experience changes both of them, even Dustin. The partners are more cautious than ever—looking out for each other, like partners should. John can sometimes have his moments, but Dustin keeps him in check.

West has taken some time off. He lives at home with his wife. Most of the crew members at *Crusher* find employment elsewhere. Some have decided to move on, while others want to stay with West until he hangs up his cap.

Dustin and John sit across from each other. The partners are investigating the crash, along with the murders onboard. From the reports of the other passengers, no one has seen anything suspicious. The deaths make sense for either of them. John is beginning to believe Dustin—that Donna's death is not suicide. After looking at the autopsies, his opinion changes. The doctor who performed it wrote: "It seems unlikely the rope would inflict such a wound. This amount of damage could *not* have been caused by the rope itself."

John walks over to the coffee maker, pouring himself a luke-warm cup. His physical appearance has changed since returning home. His face is covered with stubble, and his fingernails are longer than before.

Dustin glances at his desk phone. Next to it is a sticky note with phone numbers, from Jay to Captain West. Taking the phone off the receiver, Dustin dials a few numbers and waits for the ringing to stop.

At their new home in Delaware, Carly is working on wedding plans when she is startled by the phone. She gets out of her chair and yanks the phone off the charger. "Listen," she says firmly. "My husband and I are done with interviews. *Do not* call back unless you wanna get slapped with harassment!"

"Carly?" Dustin says, confused.

Carly recognized the man's voice. "Oh…Hi, Dustin. I'm sorry."

"It's alright. I know how you feel. No one will leave me alone either," John says, clearing his throat from across the room. "I'm sorry, Carly. *Us*. They won't leave *John* and I alone."

"Happy?" Dustin said to John. John gave a 'Yes, I am. Thank you' smile.

"How have you been?" Carly asks.

Dustin sighs, then clears his throat. "I'm alright. Trying to go back to life like it once was. How are you? How's Jay? I heard you moved."

"We're good. Living life as it should be."

"That's good. Listen, Carly. I called because I had a few ques-tions…if you don't mind."

"Go ahead," Carly says. "I'll only talk to you from now on."

"Alright," Dustin laughs slightly. "Did you or Jay see anything odd or unusual on the ship? Anyone off, or anything that didn't seem right?"

There is silence on both ends. Dustin can hear Carly drawing a breath. "Well…I didn't hear anything odd, but," Carly goes quiet.

"But what?"

"Dustin. Please promise you won't think I'm crazy when I tell you this. It's gonna sound strange, but that's what it was when it happened."

"I promise," Dustin says.

Carly tells him about the dreams she had the first night—seeing a figure hanging, but it being too blurry to make out the image. "I'm not sure," Carly says, "but I think I dreamt of Donna's death. And the Quiver woman."

Dustin kicks his feet back on his desk, throwing his legal pad on his lap in the process. "Do you usually have dreams like that, Carly?" he asks. Again, the line went quiet. "Carly, if there's something else, please tell me. Even a little bit of info could help."

Carly sadly huffs. She feels like she may cry. "I guess I'm still shaken up from it." Carly takes a quick drink. "One night, I woke up for no reason. I guess my mind told me to, and I couldn't object. I walked into the hallway, which had a spooky feeling to it. Then I saw *it.*"

Dustin writes on his legal pad. "I'm sorry. What do you mean by *it?*"

"Donna," Carly whispers.

Dustin stops writing. He freezes in his chair, not knowing what to think.

"Yes, sir. *Donna.*"

"Go on."

Carly finishes her story. She makes sure to mention what Donna told her—*find him.* Carly also mentions the red ring on her finger. Goosebumps make themselves present in his arms. Dustin is starting to put the puzzle together. Donna was married. But to whom?

"Okay." Dustin clears his throat. "Thank you, Carly. I think I got some good stuff here. Thanks for your time. Tell Jay I said hi."

"You're welcome. And I shall."

Dustin hangs up the phone. Following the conversation, Dustin does some research. Hours of research later, the only thing that comes up is paranormal activity. If that was Carly's case, what an experience!

Day turns into night. Dustin goes home to rest.

The next day.

"All units, all LA units. A call was made for 10-187. Location: 1042, Delta Ave. Any available units, please respond."

"967 responding," Dustin replies.

"Roger, 967. Be advised, it is unclear if the suspect is still in the area."

"10-4."

Dustin races to the scene. This location, both he and John knows. It is where their suspects go for an attorney—the office of Donavan Blue. Blue is a well-known and respected lawyer in LA. Both officers know him personally. They wonder what is going on here.

"LAPD!" John yells. "If you're in there, come out with your hands up!" Dustin and John have drawn their weapons. Kicking the door in, they search the office, with Dustin taking the left and John the right.

What is engraved in their minds next is horrifying.

On the floor lies a woman.

Deceased.

She has bled to death. Soon, Dustin recognizes the woman as Cassandra Ramsey, Blue's paralegal. Sitting slumped over in his chair is Donavan Blue himself. A knife sticks out of his chest, and his shirt is caked with red velvet blood, soaking paperwork on the surface of the desk. John grabs his radio while continuing to keep his lunch down. "967 requesting paramedics. There were two victims, one male and one female. Not conscious and not breathing."

"This is bad," John says to Dustin. "Really bad."

"What if our killer could be *here* in LA?" Dustin asks.

Detectives and forensics arrive at the scene. Even some of them can't believe what they are seeing. Why would somebody want to kill Blue? Why would they kill his assistant, too? The members of the forensics team answer a few other questions. Blue is stabbed nineteen times, and Ramsey twenty-two times.

At the scene, one of the detectives notices an open drawer. Files appear to be rummaged through. As the investigation goes along, detectives realize that files have been stolen. Dustin and John are relieved from the scene. They go back to the station, doing what some law enforcers dread the most.

Reports.

CHAPTER 13

WHILE THE AFTERNOON ROLLS AROUND, John stays back at the station, while Dustin is ordered to patrol the streets. "*Look for anything suspicious,*" the chief tells him. Dustin attempts to protest. He and John are partners and need to be together. Since Melaine died, Dustin has preferred a second badge.

The chief denies the appeal.

Frustrated, Dustin follows his orders.

"Good luck, Dust," John says, extending his arm. "Be safe."

Dustin grabs John's hand. "I will, brother."

The sun sets in a few hours. Patrolling the streets, Dustin keeps an eye out for troublemakers—lawbreakers. John sits at his desk. He sees the empty seat across from him and wonders if he should leave. But something tells him to stay.

Driving down the road, a silver Toyota Camry fails to stop at a red light, nearly striking a pedestrian. Dustin flicks on his lights and siren. A minute later, both cars come to a stop on a quiet road. Dustin steps out of the car, ticket book in hand. He knocks on the window.

"How you doin'?" he asks the driver.

"Alright," the driver says. The driver is a white male who has a buzz cut along with a skinny, dark goatee. The man appears to be nervous. Officer King has seen that before. Getting pulled over can be a pretty nerve-racking experience.

"Do you know why I stopped you?" Dustin asks.

The man shakes his head.

"You ran a red light and almost struck someone about a block away."

The man makes a noise with his lips. "Man, that was back there."

"I can still stop you. You got your license and registration?"

Without complaint, Dustin is given the information.

Back at the station, John has pulled some files. While he looks through them, he remembers seeing a note Blue has written: *Meeting with Charleston*. The note is dated two weeks before she died. John pounds on his keyboard. The missing files could have been Donna Charleston's. Detectives go through Blue's computer files. They find something John may like to see.

Dustin is given the proper information. As the man holds out his papers, Dustin notices a cut on the man's arm. "That's a nasty-looking scar," Dustin says.

"I got into a fight a little while ago."

"Mm-hmm." Dustin takes another look at the man. The man's face appears to be freshly shaven around his goatee. The man has his arm hidden against the middle console. "Do you mind showing your arm? You're making me a little uncomfortable." The man shows hesitation, but did. But he pivoted his arm, so you can only see the inside of his forearm. Dustin sees it immediately—a blue wave and a large, red-colored creature. His heart comes to a halt. For a moment, he froze. "Thanks," Dustin says. "I'll be right back."

John reads over his email several times. He almost can't believe what he is reading. It is a legal document Blue saved before his death: *Donna Charleston is scheduled to appear in court on January 23, 1995. The court session is for the custody battle for Donna's daughter, Ruby Charleston. The defendant is Ryan Charleston. If anything were to happen to Donna, Ruby is to be sent to a family member or a legal guardian. If the defendant (Ryan Charleston) fails to show up, Donna Charleston will be awarded full custody of her child, Ruby.*

It all makes sense. John picks up his cell phone.

Dustin sits in his patrol car. Seeing the tattoo almost makes him jump for joy. Dustin never thinks he will ever cross paths with the mysterious suspect who killed his wife in cold blood. The driver's information is processed on the computer. The driver's name is Ryan Charleston. While he sits there, Dustin thinks he heard a ringing in his ear. It seems like someone is trying to communicate with him. Dustin tries to play it off. Suddenly, a soft voice echoes in his ear. "*It's him*," the voice says. Dustin recognizes the voice. *Melaine?* He asks himself. "*It was him*," Melaine's voice says.

His arm. He knows why the man doesn't show his arm. "967, requesting backup. The suspect is pulled over, possibly a wanted fugitive." Dustin doesn't wait for a response. *I got you*, Dustin says to himself.

"Hey!" he yells. "Step out of the car!"

The driver looks confused. Trying to play it off, Dustin isn't falling for it. "I said step out of the car." The driver does not comply.

"What did I do?"

"I didn't realize I stuttered." Dustin grabs the door handle, nearly pulling the door off. "Get out of the car!"

"Dude, what the fuck!"

Dustin grabs the driver's arm. "Get out, or I'm gonna tase you!"

Everyone is gawking at the scene. Suddenly, the driver balls the gear shift in the palm of his hand, throwing it in drive. Dustin uses his other hand in an attempt to blow the clutch. His move is not quick enough. Deploying his taser on the driver does no good. "Taser deployed!" Dustin informs dispatch. "Step it up! The suspect's trying to take off on me! Heading south on Main Street!" Dustin releases his grip, almost falling to the ground.

Dustin races back to his car, chasing after the suspect, sirens piercing bystanders' ears.

John attempts to call Dustin on his cell phone again. Still no answer. Racing down the street, a call comes in over the scanner. "All available units, backup requested on Main Street. Suspect is northbound, evading police."

Just then, John sees the action up ahead. He sees Dustin fishtail after making a hard turn after the suspect. "Officer Walker responding. I have visuals on both the suspect and officer." John flicks on his lights, then pulls an insane U-turn.

With engines roaring and bystanders watching, John grabs his cell phone again and calls Dustin. Finally, Dustin answered. "I'm a little busy right now, John," Dustin says.

"I'm right behind you," John says. "I have something to tell you."

"Better make it quick."

"Donna Charleston has an ex-husband, Ryan Charleston."

There is silence. Dustin looks at the information he has. "That's who we're chasing!"

"Ryan was supposed to be in court a few weeks from now. He and Donna were battling for custody of that Ruby girl. The one from the cruise. You were right, Dust. Ryan Charleston may be our *killer*!"

"He killed Melaine, too," Dustin says.

"Get that motherfucker!" John cries.

Racing down the street, all three drivers hit 110 mph and are barely avoiding other drivers. Dustin has his pedal to the floor, surprised that his foot doesn't go through the floorboard. Right on his tail, Dustin rams Ryan Charleston's car, putting a huge dent in the back bumper. Swerving in and out of traffic, Dustin rams Ryan again. Ryan loses control of the car, swerving off the road. Dustin, too, loses control and smacks into a telephone pole. John pulls up behind the accident and runs over to Dustin's car. "Dispatch! I need that backup. Officer involved in the collision!"

Reaching for his head, Dustin unbuckles his seatbelt. The car door falls off, causing Dustin to fall out. A large cut goes along his left temple, covering his cheek. He favors his ankle.

"Dust! You alright?"

"My ankle!"

"Can you walk?"

"I don't think so."

John looks around, looking for Ryan. A few yards away, John sees smoke coming from under a small bridge. Running back to his squad car, John grabs his shotgun. "Stay here!" he calls Dustin. "I'll be right back!"

"John wait!"

John sprints down the street. He climbs down a small slope and sees the car. Its tires are bent up in the wheel stocks, the roof is caved in, and the windows are broken. The car is beyond repair. Carefully approaching, John aims his weapon. He sees no one in the driver's seat. There is a pop. A sharp pain enters John's back, thankfully, striking his protective vest. John nearly falls to the ground when he is tackled from behind. He finds himself wrestling with Ryan, dropping his shotgun in the process. Ryan pistol-whips John in the face twice before John makes an X with his arms, blocking Ryan's pistol-whip punches. With a swift motion, John's knee nails Ryan in the nuts. Ryan falls on his back, reaching in pain. John attempts to stand, but the pain in his back stops him. Another sharp pain rips through John's back. Ryan kicks the officer in the back. A bullet enters the right side of John's neck, this time missing his vest. Blood rushes from his wound, and his vision becomes blurry. Ryan stands over him. "Fuck you," John mutters.

"Johhnnnn!" Dustin cries from behind, standing on top of the bridge. Ryan spins around, and Dustin fires his weapon. Ryan reaches for his shoulder, then somehow manages to strike Dustin in the chest just above his vest, dropping him to the hard ground. Ryan flees the scene, bleeding into the stream.

"Dispatch...I'm hit...my partner is down. Requesting paramedics...I have one suspect, armed... we have been shot." Dustin finds himself unable to breathe. "I'm coming, Mel," Dustin says as everything goes black.

"All units, all units, all LA units, officers down! Officers down!"

Carly watches TV in their new Delaware home. She sees the news about Dustin and John. The story is viral. Hearing what happened to them makes Carly cry. She doesn't know them all that well, but Carly has become saddened by Dustin's story. He has already lost his wife. Now his family can be losing him. John is just as important. His family must be terrified to hear what he has suffered during the incident. Both Dustin and John are in critical condition. Now the waiting game comes into play.

The cable box shows 8:30 p.m. Carly reaches for a cup of tea on the table and wraps both hands around it. She takes a sip and suddenly begins to shake. The cold is not what makes her shake. Instead, it's fear. Flashbacks from being on the ship pop into her mind—seeing Donna in the hallway, the dreams. Thinking of everything that occurred sends chills up her spine.

Carly puts her tea back on the table and turns off the TV. She then walks to the basement door. Looking down into a dark abyss, Carly has an uneasy feeling crash down on her. Carly takes a deep breath and walks down the steps.

There is no light at the bottom of the steps. The light from the laundry room doesn't reach the end of the stairs either. So there is only darkness before her. Fear returns to her. This moment brings her back to seeing Donna in the hallway. Carly closes her eyes, finding her way to the laundry room with her hands.

Carly bumps into the sink across the washer. The brand-new overhead lights Jay installed shine above her. Carly breathes a sigh of relief. It's almost as if she is on stage with these lights.

Throwing dirty clothes into the washer, Carly pulls clean clothes from the dryer and places them on the table behind her. As she folds the clean clothes in a neat pile, a blanket of goosebumps makes itself present.

There's a sudden creaking from the door. Carly looks up, but sees nothing.

"Jay? Is that you?" Carly calls. No answer. She shrugs it off and continues with the laundry. Suddenly, another creak. Again, no one or anything. Carly thinks about investigating. She quietly inches toward the door. As she gets closer to the door, the overhead lights flicker. *That can't be,* Carly thinks; *those are new bulbs.* She fixes her attention on the lights. They flicker, then again.

"*Carly.*" A whisper.

The lights go out, leaving the room completely black.

"*Carly.*" The lights flicker back on. Hanging upside down by a rope on the lights is a woman. Her throat is deeply cut, and her face is caked with blood running down into her hair. She stares into Carly's eyes. Carly jumps back, nearly tripping on the basket of laundry behind her. Holding herself up on the washing machine, Carly can't help but stare back at the woman. "Who are you?" Carly asks in a dry voice.

In a clear whisper, the woman says, "Jenna." Carly remembers. The woman who is hanging by her feet in the tree. The woman Dustin and John find. Looking back into Jenna's eyes, Carly begins to feel lightheaded, and she wants to vomit. She can feel the color being sucked away from her skin.

"What do you want!" Carly cries. "*What do you want!*"

Jenna suddenly smiles. But it isn't Carly she is smiling at. Jenna's smile grows bigger. "She's baacckk." Carly pushes herself away from the washer.

"Who?" she asks.

Jenna points at the door with a blood-soaked arm. Her mind forces her not to look. Turning her head toward the door, Carly's heart almost sinks and explodes. Standing in the doorway is Donna. She has the same appearance as when they last met. A frown never looks so deep and intense on someone. Carly wets herself.

"Hello, Carly," Donna says. "Nice to see you again. Why haven't you done what I asked?"

"What do you mean?"

Donna shows her ring finger. The red ring is still there. "Why haven't you found him?"

Carly falls back on the washer. "The *police* will find him. They're gonna find him, Donna."

Donna lets out an ear-piercing scream and leaps at Carly's shirt collar. Donna's face turns a dark purple. Her breath reeks of rotting flesh. Now she spoke with a much hoarser voice. "I told *you* to do it."

Carly starts to cry. "But I don't know where he is."

Donna lets out another ear-piercing scream.

"Find him! Or Die!"

Donna backs into the corner of the room, climbs the wall, and disappears. Carly is face-to-face with Jenna again. This time, Jenna frowns at her. "Find him," Jenna says. "Or we will be back!"

Jenna swings herself over the light, disappearing with Donna. Carly runs upstairs, not looking back.

Running up the stairs and tripping over the last two, Carly falls to the floor and slams the door shut. Struggling to get to her feet, Carly pushes a cabinet across the door. Pushing her back against it, Carly catches her breath. When she relaxes, she walks into the living room. She puts the TV on.

Nothing happens. She pushes the ON button again. Donna's face comes on the screen; the news is behind her head. Carly wets herself again on the couch. "FIND HIM!" she yells, then vanishes. Carly sits for a long time, crying.

Carly walks up the stairs to the master's bedroom. Every step feels like a long hike up a mountain. Carly feels as if she's walking in slow motion.

In the master's bedroom, she opens the closet door. Pushing Jay's dress shirts to the side, Carly exposes a safe. Jay keeps money, valuables, and his .38 revolver inside. Loaded. Carly punches in the combination. She hears a little click, and the safe is unlocked. Carly grabs the revolver.

Carly sits on the edge of the bed. Jay's alarm clock reads 8:58 p.m. Tears fall from her cheeks to the floor. Before taking any drastic measures, Carly thinks things over. What will this do to Jay? What will her mother do if she loses her daughter? Then as Donna says, *find him or die.* She knows what Donna means by that. "Here's your wish," Carly says out loud. Cocking the gun, Carly puts the barrel in her mouth.

His Ram truck rolls down the highway, listening to 80.7 FM. Jay leans back in the driver's seat, trying to clear his mind. It has been a long day. His eyes feel heavy as he grows tired from the day. The dashboard clock reads 8:55 p.m. Turning off the highway, Jay presses down on the accelerator.

Pulling into the driveway, Jay kills the engine. He huffs, reaching over to grab his briefcase. Rubbing his eyes, he notices that the bedroom light is on and thinks nothing of it.

Inserting the key in the lock, Jay steps inside. Something feels off; Carly doesn't greet him at the door. Going upstairs, Jay finds the door ajar. Pushing the door open, Jay sees his wife with his gun in her mouth.

"Hey!" he yells. Jay grabs the barrel of the gun, ripping it from her mouth. Carly claws at his hand. Jay's gun ends up on the floor, and they scramble for it. Jay kicks it out of Carly's reach, then grabs the waistband of her shorts, pulling her away with all his strength. Jamming his knee in her back to pin her, Jay extends his arm for his revolver. When it's in his grasp, Jay releases the magazine and empties the chamber.

Tucking the revolver in his waistband, Jay picks his wife off the floor. He puts her on the bed, like he was preparing to talk to a child. Carly brings her legs up and buries her face. Jays paces around the room, trying to process what has just happened.

"Can you please explain to me what the hell you were doing?" Jay asks, shaken. Carly tells him everything. He wipes her tears as she talks. Carly thinks her husband will think she is crazy.

"I don't think you're crazy," Jay says. "We'll figure this out. Just please...don't do that again. We'll let the police handle this."

Eventually, Carly drifts off to sleep. Jay watches over her while she does so. All night, he thinks about how the love of his life almost committed suicide. Jay wonders what would have happened if he were a minute too late. But thankfully, he makes it on time. His wife is still here, still breathing.

CHAPTER 14

Friends and family gather. It has been three days since Dustin and John were shot. Tears are shed, and makeup runs down the faces of women. A slight rain falls from the colorless clouds. Trees dance with the wind, the wind hissing through their leaves.

Pastor Williams stands before the attendants. "Friends, we are gathered here today to celebrate the life of Johnathan Walker. Johnathan was a beloved friend, officer, and son. Today, let us not remember the negative, but the happy memories that Johnathan brought us."

Officer Johnathan Walker is honored with a twenty-one-gun salute. An American flag is presented to his mother and father. Roses are placed on his tombstone.

In attendance are Jay, Carly, West, and Dustin. Dustin's ankle is in a cast and on crutches. Dustin almost dies in the hospital. The bullet in his chest nearly caused him to bleed out. John is shot in the back twice, once in the neck. He dies at the scene. At the hospital, they declare his end of watch.

Soon, the crowd departs. Everyone goes their separate ways.

Back at the station, John's name is engraved on a plaque. It is for officers who died in the line of duty. Dustin gently brushes his thumb against it.

JOHNATHAN F. WALKER 1964–1995

Just a few names above:

MELAINE KING 1971–1995

Carly sits in bed, waiting for Jay to join her. The last few days have been rough. Carly is embarrassed by the actions she has tried to take. Jay has watched her like a hawk. Though he hides his gun elsewhere, Jay isn't taking any risks.

While she watches TV, the bedside table phone rings, startling her. A woman's voice is on the other end. "This is Rene Tuckerson. I'm Ruby's aunt."

"What can I do for you, Mrs. Tuckerson?" Carly asks.

"Did Ruby ever do anything strange while you watched her? Like saying anything odd or out of the ordinary?"

Carly thinks for a minute. "I don't recall."

"Well, she was sleepwalking the other day. She drew this picture, and I thought you'd like to see it. I can fax them over to you."

"Okay, here's my fax number." Carly shoots off the number. Soon, the fax machine spits out a picture. Jay thinks that for Ruby's age, the drawings are pretty good and very detailed. Ruby's artwork looks like a drawing of a ship. There is a giant red circle toward the bottom of the ship.

"What if something's down there?" Carly asks.

"It looks like she drew some sort of bomb here," Jay points out.

Jay picks up the phone.

"LAPD Headquarters, Sergeant Howard." After a minute, he hangs up the phone. He then went to a room full of officers. Like a pack of wolves on prey, they all stare at him.

"Call in SWAT. Ryan Charleston was spotted leaving Donna Charleston's residence with a Franchi SPAS-12 shotgun, along with several bottles of liquor. I got a feeling all hell is gonna break loose."

At least ten squad cars race down the highway with a SWAT truck. Rain pours heavily on the county. People watch as all the cop cars go flying by, stopping at nothing. Sergeant Howard speaks over the radio. "Alright, men. Be prepared. Ryan Charleston is considered armed and extremely dangerous. Be on the lookout for a nineteen-seventy-two black mustang. The vehicle was reported stolen last night. If you feel your life is in danger…drop him. May God be with you."

Rain soaks the officers as they move in. The units wait for Ryan to arrive home; the Mustang is not in the driveway. Witnesses report seeing Ryan living in a vacant home, off the grid if you will. A call comes over the scanner. "All units, the black mustang has been spotted. I say it again. A black mustang has been *spotted.*"

The guns are loaded and ready to fire. Adrenaline pumps through everyone. All of them prepare for the worst.

Ryan Charleston parks the stolen car in the driveway. He pops open the truck and climbs out. From the trunk, he removes his Franchi-12 shotgun. A neighbor opens their front door, sees him, then slams the door shut. Grabbing armfuls of objects, Ryan rushes to get inside the house. In the process, Ryan drops two bottles of liquor. The smell of alcohol lingers in the air, only to be washed away by the rain.

The SWAT members emerge from the truck. Taking cover behind cars, everyone knows that body armor may not be enough. A car comes screeching down the road. Coming to a sudden stop, a large man jumps from the vehicle. Detective Bryan Roman slams his car door, taking his position. Detective Roman's long goatee and long combed-back, black hair sway in the wind. His barrel chest and thick arms intimidate those who challenge him.

"You're late," Howard says.

"I hit traffic," Roman says. A few fellow officers chuckle quietly.

Police cars are formed into a U position surrounding the house. Red and blue lights blind anyone watching. The sky is almost completely dark, and the rain is not letting up. Ryan peeks out the window. "Charleston!" Roman yells. "LAPD! You're surrounded! Come out with your hands up!"

Ryan doesn't comply.

For an hour, crosshairs are aimed all over the house. A sniper lying on the roof of the SWAT truck keeps her finger on the trigger. Slowly, the rain comes to an end. All eyes are looking at Ryan. Everything is about to change.

The negotiation with Ryan is not an easy task. Nothing makes him surrender.

A bottle is thrown from a window. It catches fire in the dead grass and makes a fire wall. Another bottle is tossed, then a third, engulfing the stolen mustang in flames. Shots explode from the house. Bullets fly in both directions. More bottles are thrown, one hitting a police car, then Ryan makes a run for it out the back door.

Detective Roman chases after him.

Running like the wind, Ryan runs through backyards, jumping over fences, running homeowners over, and somehow avoiding dogs alerted by his unwelcome presence. Roman is right on his tail, his long hair and goatee flowing in the wind.

Ryan finds himself in another backyard. He has been able to avoid dogs before, but this time he isn't so lucky. A big German shepherd sinks his teeth into Ryan's arm. Trying to break free, Ryan smacks the dog's snout, but it only bites down harder. Roman runs up behind him, grabs him by the throat, picks Ryan off his feet, and slams him through a small wooden table. "Where do you think you're going, fucker!" Roman yells.

The shepherd's owner comes outside, commanding his dog to release their suspect. Bronco, the shepherd, is given a treat for his bravery. Roman then flips Ryan over and cuffs him.

"Sorry about the table," Roman says to the dog's owner.

"No worries," he says, petting Bronco. "That was awesome. Split the table in two."

Ryan hears his Miranda rights.

CHAPTER 15

DETECTIVE BRYAN ROMAN SITS ACROSS from Ryan in the interview room. His partner, Detective Thomas, stands behind tinted glass, recording the interview. Ryan's hands are cuffed to the table with shackles tight around his ankles, and his face is molded into anger and frustration. The tension in the air is so thick that you can cut it with a knife.

"Mr. Charleston," Roman says. "Do you know why you're here?"

No reply.

"Okay. Since you don't want to talk, I'll start," Roman says, opening his files. "You attempted to kill several officers of the law, threw bottles of liquor at us, and set things on fire. Do you want to talk, or should I keep going? Oh, and we also found a high-powered rifle in your residence."

No answer again. Ryan then takes a breath. "Yeah, then I got slammed through a table."

"You were resisting. I was authorized to use any force necessary."

Ryan huffs. "When can I go home?"

Detective Roman throws his head back and laughs. "Go home? With the charges you're facing, you won't be going home any time soon."

"Name some," Ryan says with a cocky attitude.

Detective Roman flips open his folder. "Let's see, shall we? Two counts of grand theft auto, assaulting an officer, careless driving, and animal cruelty. And we have believed you to be involved in not one but four murders. Two of them were police officers."

"You don't have evidence I was involved," Ryan says.

Detective Roman chuckles. "Oh, trust me. There's more than you think."

"Give me a call when you have all the proof you need," Ryan says, smiling.

Detective Roman takes a breath through his nose. Then he lightly taps the tabletop twice with his fingertips. Thomas, from behind the glass, pauses the camera, then taps on the window, back at his partner. Roman takes a handful of Ryan's hair, smacking his head off the table's surface. Roman fixes his tie as he sits back in his seat, again tapping the tabletop. Thomas turns the camera back on.

"Okay, Ryan. We're done here. I'll have an officer come get you." Roman collects his papers and calmly exits the room. Thomas powers down the camera again. Just as he does, blood begins to rush from Ryan's nose, staining the tabletop red.

Detectives Roman and Thomas meet in the hall. "You can edit that, right?" Roman asks.

"I'm on it," Thomas replies.

The next morning, Detective Roman studies as much as he can about the *Wave Crusher*. Late in the previous night, he received a fax from a woman named Carly Johnson. Roman has been in contact with her and is gathering information as he goes along. Mrs. Johnson asks if there is any way she can help with the case. Detective Roman arranges a flight from Delaware to LA for them to meet.

Detective Thomas walks through the door, a cup of coffee in hand. "You're here early," he says, looking at his watch.

"Couldn't sleep," Bryan says. "Figured I'd get a head start."

Bryan shows his partner the drawing. "I feel like something is hidden here."

"The ship?"

"*No*, the devil's ass. *Yes*, the ship."

Thomas puts his free hand on his hip. "You don't have to be so nasty about it," Thomas leans against his desk. "What are you getting at?" he adds.

"I feel like if we search the ship, we'll find something to put Charleston away for life. Notice that a murder weapon has not been found."

"Any word on the autopsy?" Thomas asks.

"Before John died, he got it back. The doctor who performed it says, "Donna Charleston was strangled before being hanged.""

"Wait, Bryan. The ship is far below the surface. What if we're too late?"

"There's only one way to find out." A smirk grows across Bryan's face. "Wanna go swimming?"

"Not really no," Detective Thomas says.

A helicopter flies to the sight of the *Wave Crusher*. From high above the water, farther down underneath, you can see this once-beautiful ship that sailed the ocean. Birds' wings slice the wind. The smell of salt in the air hits their noses, giving off a relaxed feeling and peace of mind.

Sand blows from the strong wind of the helicopter blades, looking like a desert storm. Off in the distance, Bryan sees that they have a visitor. The man stands tall, looking at the waves crashing into each other. That man is Captain West. His feet are in the water when he realizes that they have arrived.

West, Bryan, and Thomas suit up in scuba gear. On this hot day, the cool water feels good on their skin. It helps relieve the pain from the flaming sun. As soon as he is ready, Bryan throws on his mask and walks into waist-high water. His muscles scream from the sudden change in temperature, but it is nothing Bryan can't handle.

"Going in," Bryan says. "Don't forget to take your tampon out, Thomas." Bryan slides his mask on, then dives in, vanishing. Thomas and West exchange looks.

"Is he always like that?" West asks.

"Try working with him. It's worse. He'll make you cry."

Thomas and West follow Bryan's lead.

Down underwater, it is like a gorgeous world below the surface. The light from the sun gives decent visibility, and a small school of fish comes to investigate, only to find no danger. A turtle smacks a jellyfish for a late meal.

A short swim later, Bryan finds himself feet away from the ship. There it is, deteriorating and crumbling away.

Swimming through a large hole in the ship, Bryan peels away from his collages. West observes the ship he has worked on for fifteen years. What was once a wonderful vacation boat, carrying smiling people with great food and atmosphere, now lies underwater, being used as a vacation boat and eaten away by sea creatures and water damage.

Shining his flashlight through the dark rooms, Bryan slowly kicks his way around, trying to locate the spot he is looking for. There are nothing but old chairs, tables, a painting frame, silverfish, dead fish, and articles of clothing. After moving some items around and finding nothing, Bryan's gut instinct tells him to focus on the walls.

Bryan notices that the walls are tiled in this part of the ship. It looks like a bathroom. Carefully, he presses them with his thumb, waiting to see if any will break. Down on the fourth row, one of the tiles appears to be broken. Getting closer, it appears that the tile was broken once, then put back together with glue. A red flag goes up. Reaching down for his knife with his other hand, Bryan keeps the light on the suspicious tile. Prying at the square with his blade, Bryan manages to break the tile free. Dust flows back into his face. Swiping it out of the way, Bryan shines his light inside. There's something inside.

A plastic bag.

Bryan observes it. Eyeing it like it is a new discovery to man. As he attempts to exit the water-filled area, Bryan's flashlight bounces off something shiny on the floor—a shell casing—a long-caliber shell casing. A weapon has been fired on this sunken ship.

Bryan decides to swim up one more level. He finds the engine room. Piles of rubble aimlessly float. A bright shine reflects off Bryan's flashlight. Kicking his legs, Bryan locates the suspicious reflection. On the wall, Bryan spots what he thinks is a metal flask. The flask looks like it has burst, like something came out of it. And it seems as if wire has been wrapped around it.

More flashlight beams light him up like a Christmas tree—West and Thomas. Bryan holds up his discovery, then points up with his thumb, meaning to head for the surface.

Emerging, the three men study the bag. They realize that inside is a multipurpose tool. Getting a closer observation, the letters: R. B. C., are carved on its side. "My God," West says. Bryan walks over to the helicopter pilots.

"Who has the satellite phone?" he asks.

Pilot One reaches down. "I do," he says in the process.

Punching the phone numbers, Bryan continues staring at the bag. Thomas looks at him. "You calling, Dean?"

"You bet," Bryan says.

CHAPTER 16

JANUARY 28, 1996. THE NEW year has come. Eight days ago, the country celebrated the inauguration of its forty-second president of the United States. Today is the day Ryan Charleston will appear in court. Facing all kinds of charges, the whole country awaits the trials to begin. Before leaving to watch day one, Dustin reads the newspaper. Page two has an article about John.

> Officer Johnathan Walker died on December 28, 1995. Walker's life ended after chasing down a suspect with his partner. Walker and his partner were both in critical condition, but unfortunately, only his partner survived. When the chase ended, Walker was shot three times. A manhunt was launched for the suspect, who will now appear in court on several other charges. Citizens hope the jury makes the right decision. Officer Walker was thirty-one.

The article pisses Dustin off. John's family is already suffering enough. This article will only pour salt into the wound. The freedom of the press can really be a pain in the ass.

The press waits outside the courthouse, waiting for anyone involved to show up. Ryan is swarmed as soon as he hops out of the back of the squad car. Two officers escorting him push them aside.

Thomas will meet Bryan inside. He, too, is swarmed by the press. Thomas is not there to answer questions.

Bryan arrives. The press is over him like bees on a bear for stealing their honey. Bryan walks as he answers the question, not looking at any of the press members.

"Do you think Ryan Charleston will be found guilty?" one of them asks.

Bryan walks as if they are not there. "I can think whatever I want. It's not up to me. We'll have to see what the jury says. That's all I have to say." Bryan enters the courthouse. Shortly after, Jay and Carly arrive. They have come all the way from Delaware. No one tries to question them. Jay and Carly begin to think that they are forgotten about. And they are okay with that.

As the courtroom fills, Bryan and Thomas meet with Dean Rollins. Dean gets a call from Bryan that the multipurpose tool and shell casings have been found. Dean wears a dark blue suit with a black tie. His hair is neatly combed, and his face is cleanly shaved. Dean is damn good at his job. Dean graduated from Yale at the top of his class and has since been one of the best at what he did.

The men talk for a long ten minutes when Dean is called for an interview.

When he walks into the room, a woman is already standing at a podium. She has long dark brown hair, long tan legs, skinny arms and waist, and a flat chest. She speaks with a loud, clear voice.

"My name is Amanda Kirkman. I am representing Mr. Ryan Charleston. Many people are pointing the finger at him, and I will do my best to prove his innocence. I will do everything possible to make him walk free and clear his name. If you'll excuse me, I must speak to my client. Thank you."

Kirkman steps down from the podium, passing Dean on her way out. She knows Dean. She knows his reputation—his success and what he can do in the courtroom. A man taps Dean on the shoulder, indicating that it is his turn to speak. Dean is calm and collected. There is not a single nerve shivering in his body.

"Mr. Rollins!" a woman yells. "How do you feel about this trial?"

Dean takes a breath. "Personally, I think it will be fair and well-played. This is not my first rodeo, and it certainly won't be my last. For years, I've fought to put the guilty away and to keep the innocent free from bars. I can promise you I will be fighting to put Ryan Charleston behind bars for his crimes."

"How will you feel if Charleston is found not *guilty?*"

"I'm gonna cross that bridge when I come to it. It's only day one. If I lose this case, then I will have failed. In this trial, I hope to *not* lose, but that's not up to me. I could talk until I'm blue in the face, but ultimately, the jury will decide whether or not Mr. Charleston walks. A lot of people are counting on me. Losing will only let them down. The situation is worse than other people think, and I'm going to show them. Thank you for your question, but I must leave you now."

Twelve noon. Jurors take their seats. Rollins and Kirkman sit at their desks. Dean's desk is neat, while Kirkman's seems to be a little disorganized.

Dustin, Jay, and Carly sit together in the row behind Bryan and Thomas, who sit behind Dean. A door at the far end of the courtroom opens. The bailiff speaks loud and clear: "All rise for the Honorable Ronald Fitzpatrick."

Ronald Fitzpatrick is an older gentleman. His once jet-black hair now thins and changes to gray slowly. His forehead shows wrinkles, along with some freckles. He has a deep, rough voice, but he speaks clearly. Fitzpatrick is a man who plays no games. When he makes a decision, it is final. No questions about it. Dean knows this. And he knows what Fitzpatrick wants to hear.

"You may be seated," Fitzpatrick says. "Today, January 12, 2004, the state of Los Angeles versus Ryan Charleston. Before we start, Mr. Charleston. How do you plead?"

"*Not* guilty," Ryan calls out.

"Okay. First, we will hear from the defense."

Kirkman rises from her chair. She walks over to the jury, then clears her throat. "Ladies and gentlemen, today I am defending Ryan Charleston. A man who is accused of terrible crimes, including *murder*. People can always point the finger. But do they really know if my client did it? For the last few days, Ryan Charleston has been accused of murdering a police officer. I want you to ask yourself: Is there a reason he did such a thing?

"Allow me to tell you about my client. Mr. Charleston pinched and scraped to pay bills. He has never gotten the opportunity to succeed in life. Now he sits in that chair, waiting to see if he will die in prison. When the time comes for a verdict, I ask you to find my client, not guilty."

Kirkman steps away. "Mr. Rollins, you may have the floor," Fitzpatrick says. Dean takes a small sip of his water. Then he stands, adjusts his tie, and approaches the jury.

"Ladies and gentlemen of the jury, for the next couple of weeks, I am going to show you why Ryan Charleston is *guilty*." Dean holds up his hand. "Mr. Charleston is being charged for multiple crimes. Careless driving, animal cruelty, disorderly conduct, and the list goes on. But the one that sticks out the most is *murder*. This man denied all allegations against him. Is he innocent?

"When being confronted by authorities, Mr. Charleston shot an officer dead, leaving his partner to die with him." Dean points at Dustin. "That man sits right over there. Doesn't that show guilt? Though I can't say Mr. Charleston had a rough life, I ask you to focus on the *now*. I also ask you to listen carefully and pick the verdict you believe is right."

The trial goes on for two more hours. Rollins and Kirkman go back and forth with statements, objections, and throwing punches until one is down for the count. A lot of people think Dean wins this round.

At 2:30, the court is let out. Bryan, Thomas, Dean, and Dustin meet in Dean's luxurious office. Dean sits at his desk, and Thomas scopes out the plague on the wall. Bryan's in a chair with coffee in his hand, facing Dean.

"Not a bad start," Bryan says.

"I agree," Thomas says, pouring coffee. "Hopefully we can get the result we want."

"It's gonna take time," Dean says. "If we get too excited, it may not turn out well." Dean sips his coffee. Then he turns to Dustin. "Mr. King?"

Dustin looks up from the ground. He looks a little lost for a moment, almost like he doesn't get any sleep.

"Would you be willing to testify against Charleston?"

Dustin takes a long breath through his nose, then exhales. "You think it will help?"

"Absolutely," Dean says immediately. "The more people we have, the better. You have a past with Charleston. Is that correct?"

Dustin shakes his head.

"Alright. What about you two?" Dean asks Roman and Thomas. Both agree. Dean smiles. "It's settled. When the time comes, I'll call your name. Tell me everything about your experiences. Don't leave anything out. And be ready for Kirkman. She'll kick you if you go down."

"How can we be sure all our testimonies will get him convicted?" Thomas asks.

Dean's smile grows wider. "Oh, don't worry about that. I've got a surprise for that rat-bastard."

It is a new day. The sun is shining brightly, breaking the chill in the air. People in the neighborhood wear sweatshirts as they walk through the chilly wind. Maybe they are on their way to the store to pick up a few things for dinner. Or getting flowers for that special someone for their anniversary. Maybe even the ingredients to make their favorite dessert. It has been two days since the first day of the trial.

Today, Dean plans on hitting Ryan hard.

The court is in session. Judge Ronald Fitzpatrick sits in his chair, preparing himself for what is in store today. He looks up from his desk. "Mr. Rollins, you may call your first witness."

Dean stands up from his chair. "Thank you, Your Honor. I call Detective Bryan Roman to the stand." Bryan walks to the stand and takes the oath. Dean walks over and again leans on the stand. "Detective, you were the one who arrested Ryan Charleston, correct?"

"Yes, it is."

"Now, some of those charges he is facing are fleeing police and animal cruelty. Is that correct?"

"Yes, Mr. Charleston had thrown whiskey, exploding at us. After I caught up to him, I saw him abuse the dog."

"Can you tell us about that?"

"Mr. Charleston ran through someone's backyard, and then the dog bit him on the arm. He smacked at its nose to get him off. Then I took him down."

"Then you cuffed him?" Dean asks.

"Yes."

"Thank you, Detective. Nothing further."

Kirkman jumps out of her chair. "One moment, Detective. May I approach the bench?"

"Permission granted," Fitzpatrick says.

Kirkman approaches Detective Bryan. "Mr. Roman. When you arrested my client, did you happen to throw him through a table?"

Sergeant Howard's heart stops, as does Dean's.

"Yes, I did," Detective Bryan says calmly.

"Wouldn't that be excessive force?" Kirkman asks.

Detective Bryan shakes his head. "Your client was resisting arrest. And if you resist, I can do what I must to make an arrest. Throwing him through a table may have been a bit much, in your opinion, but I did what I had to do. Any other questions?"

Judge Fitzpatrick, who was resting his head on one hand, looks up. Kirkman looks stunned by his answer. That is something she hasn't thought of. "Nothing further," Kirkman says, walking back to her seat.

CHAPTER 17

JANUARY 30, 1996. KIRKMAN STANDS up from her chair. "Your Honor," she says. "I call my client, Ryan Charleston, to the stand." An officer escorts Ryan to the stand, his shackles rattle. He repeats the oath, then Kirkman approaches him.

"Mr. Charleston," she begins. "Would you please tell us about your childhood?"

"Uh, it really wasn't the best."

"Did you get along with your mother?"

"Objection!" Dean cries.

"Overruled," Fitzpatrick says. "Proceed."

"Did you get along with your mother?" Kirkman asks again.

Ryan huffs. "I thought our relationship was better," he says. "I would get in trouble for the slightest things. Dishes, my room being dirty, not taking the dog out. There was a lot."

Kirkman walks back over to her desk. "Did your mother ever hit you?"

"Objection!" Dean calls out again.

"Overruled. Continue," Fitzpatrick says.

"Yes. My mother did hit me. Later on, she kicked my dad out of the house because he tried to stop her. I never saw him again after that."

"Where is your mother now?" Kirkman asks.

There is a long pause. "Dead," Ryan finally says.

"Are you positive about that?" Kirkman asks.

Ryan nods.

Kirkman approaches the jury. "Hit by his mother. The father was forced to leave. He never had anyone to look up to. He never had anyone to teach him right. A man who was never taught the difference between right and wrong. I want you to ask yourself. Should I really find this man guilty?" Kirkman walks back and sits down.

Shortly after, the court is dismissed for the day. Everyone goes home for the night, wondering if Ryan can really be found *not* guilty. Dean realizes then that he has to throw a harder punch if he wants to win. However, little does anyone else know about his surprise for Ryan.

Ryan has been on trial for an entire week. Kirkman has been fighting to keep Randy out of prison, while Rollins does everything he can to put Randy away for life, calling witnesses and hitting him hard with testimonies. Little does Randy know, Dean has a few more tricks up his sleeve.

"Mr. Rollins, the floor is yours," Fitzpatrick says.

"Thank you," Dean says. "Your Honor, I'd like to call another witness."

"Please do," Fitzpatrick replies.

Dean buttons his suit coat. "I call Megan Charleston to the stand."

Ryan nearly jumps out of his chair, spinning around and trying to look for her. Detective Roman spots her and thinks, *Dean, you smart son of a bitch!* Megan Charleston walks to the stand. She is wearing a light pink dress with her hair down, white shoes, and a little American flag pin near her heart. She sits down at the stand, takes the oath, and prepares for the questions. Dean moves a few files around in front of him before approaching. Fixing his tie, he approaches.

"Mrs. Charleston, for the record, could you please state how you know the defendant?" Dean says.

Megan Charleston shakes her head. "I'm his mother, Mr. Rollins."

Everyone leans back in their seats and quietly gasps. Fitzpatrick perches up in his chair as well. A look of fear comes over Ryan's face.

"Mrs. Charleston, could you please point out your son to the court?" Dean asks.

DEVIN SCHLOTTMAN

With no hesitation, she points directly at Ryan, who is probably shitting his pants at the moment. Dean puts a hand up to his lips, turns, walks back to his desk, and opens a file. "Mrs. Charleston? Are you aware that your son told us that you were deceased?"

Megan Charleston looks at her son with disbelief. Her eyes begin to water as she processes what she is told. "No, I was not aware. I don't know why he would say that. I've been trying to contact him for a while now. He refuses to talk to me."

Dean shakes his head. "Well, Mrs. Charleston. I'm sorry to tell you that he did say that. May I ask you a personal question?"

"You may."

"How did you and Ryan get along when he was a child?" Dean asks, walking toward the middle of the room.

"My son and I did have our moments. But I did love him very much. I was always trying my best to encourage him, but he seemed like he didn't care. I tried to help him with all his problems as best I could. Sometimes, he'd get so furious, he'd hit me. One time, he was struggling with something. I think it was homework. He kept saying he was stupid, and I told him, 'Don't talk like that.' He ended up throwing a lamp at me, hitting me. I did punish him for that, but I would never lay a finger on him."

A quiet gasp comes from the audience. Dean shakes his head, placing his hand back on his mouth. "Ma'am, I'm sorry to tell you this. But your son lied." Dean flips through papers. "Your son was asked by Miss Kirkman and I quote,

Did your mother ever hit you?

Yes. My mother did hit me. Later on, she kicked my dad out of the house because he tried to stop her. I never saw him again after that.

Where is your mother now?

Dead.

"Your Honor." Dean points to Ryan. "Ryan Charleston lied under oath. He said that his mother hit him. Not true. He said his mother was deceased. And there she sits. Alive and well. I ask that you charge the defendant with perjury."

"The motion to file perjury to the record is noticed. And the motion is granted!" Fitzpatrick calls out.

Megan Charleston buries her face in her hands. A waterfall comes out of her eyes, and in total, she shakes her son, whom she did love but who lied about her. Dean walks over, putting a hand on her shoulder. "I know this is hard, Mrs. Charleston, but I have to ask one more question. Did you kick your husband out of the house when Ryan was a child?"

"Objection!" Kirkman yells.

"Overruled!" Fitzpatrick screams.

Megan Charleston shakes her head aggressively, not even being able to look up as she continues to cry. Dean pats her on the shoulder. "Let the record show that Mrs. Charleston is shaking her head 'no' in response to the question. She is unable to speak because of the pain her own son has brought upon her. Thank you, Mrs. Charleston. Nothing further, Your Honor."

Detective Roman, Detective Thomas, and Dustin want to clap as Dean goes back to his seat. Megan Charleston exits the courtroom, devastated. Her cries can be heard from down the hall.

Dustin is helped to the stand. His ankles are weak, and his chest is aching from the removed bullet. Deep down inside, he doesn't want to do this. Dean finally encourages him to testify the night before. Dustin hopes that his testimony will put the man who killed John and Melaine away for good.

"Officer King." Dean approaches the witness. "Just recently, you were admitted to the hospital?"

"Yes," Dustin says quietly.

"Could you please tell us about that?" Dean sees a look on Dustin's face. "If it doesn't bother you, officer," Dean adds.

Dustin draws a slow breath. "I pulled Mr. Charleston over prior to the chase. Then my late partner, Officer John Walker, discovered something about him."

"Objection!" Kirkman yells.

"Overruled."

"What was it your fellow officer discovered?" Dean asks.

Dustin huffs. "Some files. Something that could have gotten the defendant in a lot of trouble."

"Officer King, had you come along with Mr. Charleston in the past?"

"It's possible."

"Objection! The witness is making up accusations!" Kirkman calls out.

"Ms. Kirkman—" Fitzpatrick begins.

"*Making up accusations?*" Dustin interrupts. "I'm not making anything up! I recognized your client by his tattoo." Dustin looks at Ryan. "You wanna know how I know? Do you remember killing my wife in cold blood!"

"I didn't kill any cop," Ryan says.

"Bullshit!" Dustin screams. "Months ago, I was at your house! My wife! She chased you down an alley, and you shot her!"

"Objection!"

"Sustained. Mr. King, calm yourself down," Fitzpatrick says.

"No! I won't calm down! Not until I see this bastard locked up!"

"Fuck you!" Ryan yells.

Dustin's hands slam down on the stand. "Go fuck *yourself*! You put me in the hospital! You shot my partner dead! You took my wife away! Be thankful you're still breathing! You worthless piece of shit!"

Fitzpatrick pounds his gavel. "If you don't calm down, Mr. King, I will hold you in contempt!"

Dustin becomes quiet. His face is red, with eyes watering and waiting to burst. The painful memory of his fallen wife is brought to his attention again.

"Your Honor," Dean says, slightly shaken. "I have nothing further. Thank you, Mr. King." Dustin steps down from the stand, refusing help from two bailiffs. Tension lingers in the air. Judge Fitzpatrick calls a recess.

Dean presents an evidence box to the jury. Slipping on rubber gloves, Dean reaches inside. He pulls out a plastic bag, holding it out to the jurors. "This, ladies and gentlemen, is a multipurpose tool, a shell casing, and an AR15 high-powered rifle. This evidence was found by Detective Bryan Roman himself. Little did anyone know it was hidden on the now-sunken ship.

"While in testing, not one but *two* traces of blood were found. Blood from Donna Charleston and a young lady named Jenna Quiver. Also, a metal flask was found. After testing, we discovered residue that is found in explosives such as bombs." Dean puts the evidence back and then removes his gloves. "Before his death, Johnathan Walker did some digging. Ryan Charleston was married and had a child. His marriage starts to unravel several years later, and the couple decides to go their separate ways. However, Ryan's wife, Donna, wanted full custody of their child. There's more. At this time, I'd like to call Ryan Charleston to the stand."

Ryan is brought back to the stand. "Mr. Charleston, shortly after you and your wife separate, you find out a friend of yours is also getting divorced. Is that right?"

"Maybe."

Dean knows that Ryan is playing a game.

"So your child has a friend at school. Your buddy tells you this news. And you get angry. He might lose his child. And that doesn't sit well with you."

"You don't know that," Ryan says, hostile.

"Later on, you find out that your ex-wife and your friend's ex-wife-to-be happen to be going on the same cruise."

"Objection!"

"Be careful, Mr. Rollins," Fitzpatrick adds.

"You knew that if you could get on that ship, you could end everything that was making your life a living hell. If you eliminate the problem, you will be able to get your child. So you snuck on the ship, snuck down to the engine room, and planted a makeshift bomb on the wall. You killed Donna by strangling her with a rope and then hanging her to make it look like suicide. Shortly after, you found Jenna Quiver and executed her the same way, but then hung her in a tree to throw everyone off. Then, when the people performing their own investigation were getting rescued by the Coast Guard, you pulled out your assault rifle and fired at them. You knew that if they got off that island alive, you would spend the rest of your days in prison! Then not only did you commit murder on that ship, you made it a personal mission to execute Donavan Blue and Cassandra Ramsey. Because if they showed a judge she was dead, documents would take your child from you."

"This is an argument!" Kirkman says.

Fitzpatrick smacks his gavel again. "One more wrong word, Mr. Rollins, and I'll hold *you* in contempt!"

"Mr. Charleston, deny it all you want, but the truth is out. Nothing further."

The room is quiet. A pin can be heard hitting the floor. Dean calmly walks back to his desk, taking a drink of water.

Judge Fitzpatrick locks his hands together in front of his hands and huffs. "Mr. Charleston," he says. "I'm giving you the opportunity to speak for yourself."

Ryan sits with his head down, his chin touching his chest. Kirkman walks up to him, and she whispers in his ear. Probably telling him to speak, not asking, *telling*.

"Mr. Charleston?" Fitzpatrick asks.

"No, Your Honor."

CHAPTER 18

NEWS OF THE TRAIL HIT channels everywhere within minutes. Hundreds of thousands of newspapers are printed. The caption reads: CHARLESTON GUILTY? People all over the country start to believe that Ryan is the culprit.

Dean stands at the podium the next morning. The press members shove and push each other. From the look of him, Dean is a confident man.

"Mr. Rollins," a voice says. "With Charleston not testifying, does that make you think he admits his guilt?"

"No question about it," Dean says. "A lot of people thought he was guilty from the beginning. I'm not sure whether or not Ryan knows he just hurt himself in the jury's vote."

"Do you know what sentence is in place?" someone else asks.

"I am aware of the punishment. However, I was asked not to share that information, and I'm going to respect those orders."

"With everything that has gone on in this trial, how do you feel?"

"I feel very good. But like I said from the beginning, I can say what I want to say and think what I want to think. Only the jury will decide the fate of everything. I can assure you, though, that if Charleston is found *not guilty*, the devil will be dancing."

Today is the final day of the trial. Both Kirkman and Rollins will present closing arguments and see who wins this bout. Large puddles of water bundle up outside, creating mud pits. Everyone takes shelter inside their homes, some in the courtroom. Dean hopes that today is the last time he will see Ryan.

The Honorable Ronald Fitzpatrick is about to hear the closing arguments.

Then, it's the jury's turn.

Amanda Kirkman takes the floor. "Ladies and gentlemen. For the last few weeks, I have tried to convince you that my client, Ryan Charleston, is not guilty of the charges against him. Was it the fact that he had no one to help him with everything he was dealing with that caused him to commit these crimes? Did not having a father figure do this? No one is perfect. Even with all the evidence against my client, I hope you see past all of that and find him *not* guilty."

Kirkman takes a seat.

Dean takes a sip of water, then approaches the jury.

"Ladies and gentlemen of the jury. I stand before you today, asking you to do one thing. To find Ryan Charleston *guilty* of all the charges against him. Not only did his attorney just lie about his father, she is trying to help a clearly guilty man walk free. Ladies and gentlemen, with all the evidence, testimonies, conspiracies, and lies, personally, this should be an easy decision.

"I am not trying to persuade you in the wrong direction. But think about it. The defendant had a plan for nearly all his crimes. He even lied under oath, making his mother burst into tears. And he didn't even prove his innocence on the stand.

"First, he killed the mother of his child, making it look like suicide. He killed the soon-to-be ex-wife of a childhood friend in a rather gruesome way—slitting her throat and then hanging her like an animal in a slaughterhouse. There is evidence that he killed two attorneys, afraid they would find something and then he would lose his child. And he took the lives of not one but two well-respected police officers.

"I hope, ladies and gentlemen, that after everything is presented, you will find Ryan Charleston guilty." Dean goes back to his seat.

While the jury makes their decision, everyone goes outside for fresh air. Everyone shields themselves with umbrellas.

"So, Dean," Jay says. "What's gonna happen if Ryan's not guilty of murder?"

Dean huffs, his breath looking like he has exhaled cigar smoke. "Either way, if the murder conviction doesn't get him, the other charges will. Like animal cruelty and assaulting officers. Stuff like that. Fines will also be enforced."

"So either way, he's doing jail time?" Jay asks.

Dean shakes his head. "If he somehow avoids the other charges, he'll do an automatic five years for perjury. The bright side is that he can get convicted on all charges and never walk out. Even being convicted of murder."

"You said you knew one of the possible punishments?" Bryan asks.

"Indeed, I do." Dean looks around. "Life without parole, on top of all the other charges."

They wait. "The other?" Carly asks.

Dean's face shows a blank expression. Suddenly, his cell phone rings. Walking away, Dean answers. He comes back, walking past them. "We have a verdict."

The seats in the courtroom fill rapidly. Fitzpatrick makes his way to his chair, and the jury takes their seats once more. The heavy rain smacks on the windows. Fitzpatrick puts on his glasses. "Will the defense please rise and face the jury?" Both stand. "Has the jury reached a verdict?"

A short, skinny man rises from his chair. "We have, Your Honor." The juror removes a piece of paper from his pocket. Fitzpatrick looks at his files.

"On the count of animal cruelty, how do you find the defendant?"

"Guilty."

"On the count of assaulting a police officer, how do you find the defendant?"

"Guilty."

"On the counts of perjury and careless driving, how do you find the defendant?"

"Guilty, Your Honor."

"On six counts of second-degree murder, how do you find the defendant?"

"We, the jury, find Ryan Charleston on six counts of second-degree murder…"

It goes quiet. Dean's heart screeches to a halt. "Guilty as charged."

Kirkman hides her face in her hands. Ryan's head drops into his chest. Everyone wants to jump from their chairs and cheer. While everyone holds their composure, Judge Fitzpatrick inhales through his nose and then exhales.

"Is this your verdict, so say you all?" he asks.

"We do, Your Honor," the jurors say at once.

"The jury has spoken. Ryan Charleston, due to the graphic nature of this case, I am left with no choice. I hereby sentence you to death by lethal injection. Jurors, thank you for your service. You are dismissed. Court adjourned." Fitzpatrick smacks his gavel. Finally, the trial is over. News spreads like wildfire soon after Fitzpatrick stands to exit the room.

Two muscular deputy sheriffs escort Ryan down the steps of city hall. The news media swarm him as he is soon taken to the county jail to live out his life until the lethal injections are scheduled.

Jay and Carly begin to walk to their car while their friends remain. Dustin stands at the bottom of the steps with Dean.

The patty wagon is warming up while the driver waits for his next passenger. Ryan curls his wrists so his cuffs are tucked away. Dustin notices that he seems to be fiddling with them. In one sudden motion, Ryan removes his left hand from the cuff, reaching for one of the deputies' firearms. There is a brief struggle. "Gun!" Dustin cries. Ryan shoots the deputy in the hand as he attempts to shield himself. The second deputy tries wrestling Ryan to the ground, but it is unsuccessful. Ryan stumbles down the last few steps. Dean steps in front of him. Dustin shoves him out of the way, clutching his crutch in one hand and raising it above his head.

Dustin smacks Ryan in the back. It does little. Ryan whips Dustin in the cheek with the stolen firearm. Dustin feels the pain run through his foot as Ryan stomps on his cast. As Dustin cries in pain, he grabs the barrel of the gun. Grabbing hold of Ryan's wrist,

Dustin bends it as far as he can until he hears a pop. Ryan drops the weapon as he yelps. Dustin sees Ryan's fist fly and land on his cheek, then grabs him by the neck. "Your wife can't save you now, bitch!"

Dustin's pain suddenly vanishes. Rage accompanied an adrenaline pulse through him.

Dustin grabs Ryan's orange jumpsuit, screaming in his face. Balling up his fist, Dustin lands several punches to Ryan's stomach and face. Ryan trips over the steps with Dustin hot on his tail, letting out cries of pain. Like an anaconda, Dustin wraps his arm around Ryan's neck. Ryan claws at Dustin's hands and face. Dustin is not going to let go. If he chokes Ryan to death on these steps, so be it.

Ryan shifts his body. Dustin feels the rubber part of his dropped crutch strike his face. Then a second and third time. The pain forces Dustin to reach for his skull. Ryan tosses the crutch and makes a run for it. "No!" Dustin yells.

BOOM!

Dustin looks up.

Ryan wipes blood from his back.

BOOM! BOOM!

Carly Johnson, with her high heels and a face full of makeup, stands just feet away from the convicted killer. "Stay down!" Carly orders. Ryan observes his blood-painted hand. He shares his looks with Carly. A demon's smile covers Ryan's face, his teeth red. He lets out a hysterical laugh. Ryan charges Carly.

BOOM! BOOM!

Ryan falls to his knees, falling on his face. Carly carefully approaches the killer. She takes a pause to realize what she has done. Ryan lies on the ground, where the last two shots enter his body. One on the shoulder and one in the chest. The demon's smile on Ryan's face is gone. Blood coats the concrete underneath him. Carly lowers the weapon. She spots Dustin on the steps, looking at her, and is amazed that she has found it in her to take action, especially in a situation like this. Carly looks back at Ryan. She can see life slowly leaving his body.

"That was for Donna. And Melaine."

Officers surround the city hall with flapping police tape. Carly is taken in for a brief questioning with an attorney from the DA's office. Several witness testimonies state seeing Carly take action when Ryan stole the deputies' firearm.

The DA speaks.

"The events that took place today were tragic. For those who do not know, after Ryan Charleston was sentenced, Mr. Charleston broke free from custody and wrecked more havoc. After an investigation, it was discovered that Mr. Charleston had stolen a paper clip from his attorney's desk and used it to pick at his cuffs until he managed to break free. Mr. Charleston fought to get away until a brave civilian stopped him. At this moment, Mr. Charleston is pronounced dead. The civilian will remain anonymous for privacy reasons. Before we get to questions, the civilian who shot and killed Mr. Charleston will not be facing any charges." The DA looks up from her papers. "Any questions?"

"What will you do to assure the public that this won't happen again?"

"I will do everything to the best of my ability to make sure an incident like this never happens again. I have two injured deputies. They will recover, but this should not have happened."

The questions end shortly after they start. Everyone involved with this case wants to move on and live their lives, though the memories from this will live on forever.

CHAPTER 19

DUSTIN AND DEAN SIT AT the bar, watching a baseball game. Rather than a beer, Dustin sinks his teeth into a fresh plate of nachos and a Coke. In front of Dean is a half-drank beer. Both simultaneously cheer as the Dodgers score a run on a double.

"Sorry, we're late," Jay says, grabbing Dustin's shoulder. Dustin sticks out his hand with a big grin on his face.

"Right on time," Dustin says. He gives Carly a hug.

"It is gone!" the announcer screams. The whole bar yells with joy.

The gang talks for hours. Each of them has new adventures in their lives. Dustin is thriving as an officer after battling his injuries. Dean has been considering running for DA. Jay and Carly grow even closer together.

The group consumes lots of beer and shares many laughs. The adventure they have been through together will forever bond them as friends.

All hands on death.

ABOUT THE AUTHOR

DEVIN SCHLOTTMAN CURRENTLY RESIDES IN Pennsylvania with his family. He enjoys reading, writing, drumming, listening to music, watching sports, and spending time with his loved ones in his spare time.

Printed in the USA
CPSIA information can be obtained
at www.ICGtesting.com
CBHW031621150824
13252CB00011B/389